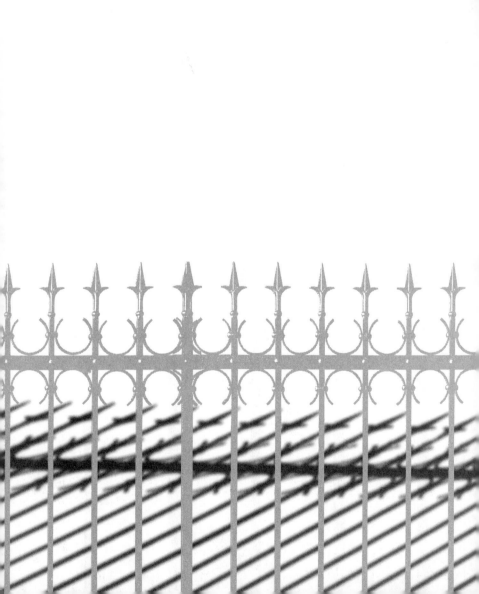

WACKO ACADEMY

FAITH WILKINS

Arundel
PUBLISHING

WACKO ACADEMY

Copyright © 2012 by Faith Wilkins

Book design by Christian Fuenfhausen

All rights reserved.

For information:

Arundel Publishing,

P.O. Box 377, Warwick, NY 10990

ArundelPublishing.com

ISBN   978-1-933608-80-8

First Edition: 2012

Printed in the United States of America

10 9 8 7 6 5 4 3 2 1

WACKO ACADEMY

PROLOGUE

I stared out the window, head swimming from the height. The voices from behind me had grown louder, angrier. There wasn't much time left. I had to jump now. My friend's life depended on it. Heck, *my* life depended on it, but fear seemed to have frozen every muscle in my body. I was completely immobilized.

The others stared up at me, wondering why I hadn't done anything yet. I was holding them all up, compromising everything. Maybe they would have to leave me. No, I couldn't let that happen. This was my only chance.

Footsteps joined the voices now. I closed my eyes, wondering how it could have come to this . . .

THE NEW KID

I have to admit, when I entered the school building on that first day of eighth grade, I was nervous. And I mean really nervous. Like the heart-pounding, pulse-racing, sweat-inducing kind of nervous. I had no idea what to expect. This was my last year in middle school and I wanted to make it count. Without a doubt, this would be my toughest year.

I took a deep breath and started for my homeroom, Gamma 17, Mrs. Ellingham's room. I walked in, scanning for a familiar face. Spotting my best friend, I dashed toward her. "Malerie, hi!"

"Lily, I'm so glad you're in my class!" she exclaimed.

"Me too!" I squealed. We embraced each other, giggling with delight.

"Hello, girls," I heard a quiet voice say. I would've known that voice anywhere. It was Louis Jennings, another good friend.

"Hey, Freckle Face. What's up?" I asked him.

"Ah, nothin'. Just glad to see people I know," he greeted me cheerfully. We all stood around chatting about what we'd done during the summer.

After a while, I noticed a boy lounging by the window who appeared to be very bored. His golden brown skin was smooth, almost flawless. The breeze from outside gently blew through his dark curly hair. He wore a black leather jacket. Peeking out from under the vintage jacket was a white polo shirt. Instead of the usual guy-wear of baggy pants, he had on jeans that fit him quite well. For a change I did *not* catch a glimpse of any polka-dotted undergarments. To top it off, he had on what had to be hundred-dollar sneakers. He was twirling a pair of designer sunglasses while he gazed out the window. The boy must have noticed me staring, because he slowly turned around to meet my curious gaze. I quickly looked away.

"Hey, Mal. Who's tall, dark, and I'm-So-Handsome over there?" I whispered, pointedly turning my back on the boy model.

Malerie had been talking to Louis about her crazy vacation. She stopped mid-sentence.

"Oh, that's the new kid, Dustin Chandelle. Rumor has it he moved here from Florida," she explained. "He's cute, right?"

I didn't answer. He may have been cute, but something about him just wasn't right.

Mal continued to talk to Louis while I stole a quick glance at Dustin. He was looking me up and down like he was checking me out or something, a little smirk on his face. There was something arrogant about it, like he already had me all figured out. I frowned. Just who did this kid think he was? As if to answer my unspoken question, he winked at me. Apparently he thought pretty highly of himself. Ugh. I felt like punching that annoying grin off of his handsome face. I surprised myself by smiling at the thought of hitting him.

Dustin raised an eyebrow and cocked his head, as if to ask what I was grinning about. This time it was my turn to wink.

"Okay, kids. You know the drill. Find a desk and take a seat," said Mrs. Ellingham.

I chose a desk between Malerie and Louis. Unfortunately, Dustin sat at a desk right in front of me. I glared at him. He pretended not to notice.

The teacher explained what we would be doing in ELA this year. She handed out a schedule for the school day. Everyone groaned at the hot lunch selection, rib sandwiches. Nobody knows what the meat in those sandwiches is made of. Rolling my eyes, I pretended to gag. Mal giggled and pretended to gag too.

Mrs. Ellingham calmly waited until the groans stopped. She handed out textbooks and workbooks. This started the groans all over again.

It was the same in history and math. Only in math, Mr. Stallsberg made us do some equations and gave us a really thick packet to complete for homework. To my great annoyance, Dustin seemed to be in all of my classes so far. However, there was one class I knew he wouldn't be in with me: Japanese. The people that went to Japanese class had been taking it since sixth grade, so there was no way he could be there. Not unless he just happened to have been studying Japanese for the last two years.

I entered the classroom with a bounce in my step, and said hi to all my friends. I was thrilled to be reunited with them and relieved to be away from Dustin.

"I wonder who the teacher is this year," I mused. "Or what field tri-" My smile faded and I gawked at the person walking in. The class turned their heads to stare at the newcomer.

Just then, our new teacher appeared on the television at the front of the room. "Hello, class. I've heard great things about you guys." She paused to look at the class list. "Seems that we have a transfer student. Dustin Chandelle, is it?"

"Yes, ma'am," Dustin replied.

His voice didn't surprise me, smooth and a little conceited. Like that smirk of his.

I was sitting there seething, watching Dustin kiss up to the teacher, when Ella tapped me on the shoulder.

"Lily," she whispered, "you've been staring a hole into that guy's head for like twenty minutes. We're supposed to be reading page 47 in our textbooks now, so get to it!"

I started reading, grateful that she had snapped me out of it. This is why she's one of my best friends. She's always got my back.

I made sure not to look at Dustin for the remainder of the period, even though I occasionally felt his eyes on me, sending chills down my spine. Somehow I knew that if I looked up, that stupid smirk would greet me. So I kept my eyes firmly on my work.

When class was finally over, I hurried to my locker to put

my binders and pencils away before lunch. While I worked on my combination, someone came up from behind me.

"I couldn't help but notice you staring at me back there," With a startled yelp, I jumped about a foot off the ground. I whirled around to back up against my locker.

"Whoa, too close," was all I could muster.

Dustin heard me and backed away. "Excuse me for asking, but did I do something wrong?"

I looked him over. He seemed genuinely concerned. I mean, I would be too if it were my first day at a new school and already somebody was staring daggers at me. Maybe I had made the wrong assumptions. This wouldn't be the first time.

I sighed. "No, I'm just having a weird day. It has nothing to do with you, really. Speaking of weird . . . don't take this the wrong way, but don't you think it's kind of strange that we're in all the same classes?"

He shrugged. "I dunno. No offense, but I didn't really notice. Anyway, sorry you're having a weird day. To tell you the truth, I'm not really having that normal of a day either."

His warm chestnut eyes bored into mine as if he saw right through me. Then he let me have the final blow. "Sorry if I made it worse."

I froze, mortified. He walked away, leaving me still frozen by my locker, feeling like a total jerk.

By recess, I was still feeling terrible about the way I had acted with Dustin.

I sat on the bleachers next to my chatting friends, but I didn't join the conversation. Instead, I swept my eyes across the field, looking for him. Why? I wasn't exactly sure. I soon found him sitting in the middle of a mob of giggling girls. They were apparently laughing at some joke he'd made. Dustin seemed completely at ease with being the center of attention.

Crossing my arms, I turned away, not believing that I had been so ashamed. He was just like I thought, egotistical and arrogant. Or was he? Maybe I was just making assumptions again.

"Uh, Lily, are you okay?" asked Ella.

I had been so lost in my own thoughts that I hadn't noticed when my friends had stopped talking to stare at me.

"Yeah. Why?" I answered.

"Well, you seem kind of spacey. What's on your mind?"

I looked around at the sea of eyes focused on me. I bit my lip, wondering if I should tell them. The problem seemed so minor. They would all probably just laugh at me.

So I simply said, "Nothing. I'm just tired."

Ella gave me a look like she didn't believe me, but didn't press the subject. Everyone went back to their conversations.

Now I jumped down and took a walk along the field. I wasn't sure why this was bugging me so much. I thought about the way he had looked at me in our first class. If I didn't know any better, I would say he was sizing me up. Why would he be doing that? He didn't know me. I felt like I was missing something here. Perhaps he had simply been looking for a friend. He really wasn't going to have any trouble there. The boy was downright handsome. The popular kids probably had a place at their lunch table reserved just for him. Besides, a fair number of good-looking boys turn out to be total arrogant jerks. Dustin seemed to be no better than the rest.

This whole thing was driving me crazy. Suddenly I changed direction and headed for Dustin and the mob of giggling girls. I would get down to the bottom of this now. If this bothered me so much, then what better way to solve the annoying problem than to go directly to the source?

As I got closer, I started having second thoughts. What if this was a mistake? What if I just ended up looking like a complete idiot, making a big deal out of nothing? But by the time I had decided to turn around and walk away, it was too late. I was already standing in front of him. It would look really dumb if I just turned and left.

"Um . . . Dustin, can I talk to you for a minute?" I asked timidly.

One of the giggly girls mumbled that I should get in line. Dustin stared at me quizzically for a minute, a hint of a snide smirk starting to show. "Sure." He stood up and followed me away from the now-angry bunch of girls.

"So what did you wanna talk to me about? Didn't you want, like, nothing to do with me?" he asked.

"Did it really seem that way?" I asked, eyebrows slightly scrunched.

He nodded.

"Oh." I shoved my hands in my pockets. "Well, sorry if I made you feel that way. Guess I was being kind of a jerk. I'd like to have a fresh start, if that's okay with you?"

Dustin studied me, as if he was making sure I was truly sorry. He must have decided that I was, because a wide grin spread across his face. This grin was playful and sweet. It made him look even better than before. I fought back a smile, still not fully trusting him.

"Yeah, you were kind of being a jerk," he agreed.

I gave him a little shove. He laughed. I couldn't help but laugh along with him.

"I think a fresh start would be nice," he continued. "My name's Dustin. And yours is . . . ?" He held out his hand as if to give me a handshake.

I glanced down at his waiting hand and back at him. With a smile I accepted his handshake, finding his hand to be quite firm.

"Lilith Mason, but you can call me Lily, or Lil. Whatever you prefer."

So I spent the rest of recess getting to know him better. This was unusually easy to do. I had only just met him, yet it was like we were already friends. I ended up forgetting every cautious feeling I'd had about him. When recess was over, I surprised myself by feeling sorry.

"Time to go back to class." Dustin said solemnly.

He looked sorry too. I nodded and hurried to get inside.

WATCHED

As the weeks progressed, Dustin and I became pretty good friends. He turned out to be kind and intelligent. He loved music almost as much as I did. In addition to that, he was a bookworm like me. The boy seemed to be perfect. *Too perfect*, a voice said in my head. I ignored it, pushing it to the back of my mind. However, a part of me was determined to find a flaw.

"So, Dustin, what are you not good at?" I asked at recess one October day.

He turned his head toward me with his eyebrows raised. "What do you mean?"

"Well, you seem to be good at a lot of things, and I was just wondering if there was anything that you couldn't do that well," I said quickly, suddenly embarrassed.

He frowned in thought. "Let me think . . ." he said slowly. "I was never good at baseball. Or anything having to do with a ball and a bat, for that matter."

I smiled. It was the same for me too.

"Any more questions?" he teased.

Actually, yes there were. I let out a flood of questions,

asking why he had moved from Florida, if he had any brothers or sisters, and why he wore such expensive clothes. The minute I said those words, I wished that I hadn't. A dark shadow clouded his face.

"You don't have to tell me anything if you don't want to." I said quietly.

He shook his head, admitting that he just hadn't talked to anyone about his family before. He went on to tell me that he had moved here from Florida because of his dad's new job. No, he didn't have any biological siblings, although he had adopted brothers and sisters that dropped in from time to time. As for the stylish attire, his dad's job was paying him well, so his father insisted that he wear good-quality clothing. Dustin hadn't really wanted to wear it.

"Anything else you want to know?" he asked sincerely.

I apologized before I told him that yes, I did have one last thing to ask. What about his mom? Not once in this whole conversation had he mentioned her.

"My mom . . . passed away when I was seven," he said sadly.

Oh. I didn't know what to say.

"It might seem kind of stupid, but I keep a picture of her in my pocket. To remember her."

I looked up. "Really?"

He nodded. "Stupid, right?"

I shook my head. "Not at all. May I see it?"

He reached into his jacket pocket and carefully took out a small photo. With slightly hesitant hands, he gave it to me.

"She's so pretty."

And she was. She had the same shining eyes as Dustin. Her smile was so bright and full of life; it could make even the saddest person happy. Her dark wavy hair cascaded down her shoulders. Around her neck, she wore a beautiful diamond necklace with a shiny gold horse pendant dangling from the middle. She held a blossoming flower in her hands. Her rich brown skin seemed to shine in the sunlight.

I looked over at Dustin staring at the picture. He and his mother were so alike it was startling. He had her hair, eyes, and dazzling smile. When he stood in the sunlight, his skin seemed to shine just like hers.

"You look so much like her," I told him.

"My dad tells me that a lot," he said softly. He cleared his throat. "This picture was taken about a year before she died."

"Do you want to tell me about her?" I asked, still staring at the picture.

"Well, I don't really remember much," he said slowly. "But I do remember her stories. They were about parallel worlds and time travel. You know, science fiction stuff. Nobody could tell a story like she could." He stopped. "That's all I can remember, really. That and her smile."

I didn't know what to say. His mom sounded awesome. I knew he didn't want my pity, but I couldn't help feeling sorry for the guy. Dustin seemed to have been close to his mom. I tried to imagine life without my own mom and grimaced at the thought. That would be terrible. There was no way I could truly understand what he was going through, but I did understand that his life couldn't be that easy without one of his parents.

Before he could say any more, the bell rang. I gave the picture back to him. We walked back inside in silence.

I was still thinking about him when I got off the bus that afternoon. Normally, I would be making the short trek home with my neighbor Chase, but he had not been in school. He's one of those kids who skip school just to skip school.

Suddenly the little hairs on the back of my neck rose. I stopped walking for a second. Something in the air had changed. I got the strange feeling that someone else was there with me. But the bus was long gone and there was nobody in sight. I glanced around. Nothing. Just an empty road lined with silent houses.

Clutching my backpack a little tighter, I started to walk again. Ignoring the chills rolling down my spine, I kept a brisk pace. My house was only a block away, but now it seemed way farther. I thought I heard another pair of feet moving behind me. I whirled around, thinking that maybe I could catch them by surprise. Nothing.

Frustrated now, I began to trot down the street. Maybe I was going crazy. Maybe not. Either way, I had to get home. Now.

By the time I finally reached the front door of my house, I was out of breath. I had broken into a sprint once I caught sight of the house. I turned one last time, but I still didn't see anything. With a relieved sigh, I took my copy of our house key out of my pocket, unlocked the door, and went inside.

AN UNEXPECTED VISITOR

The next day, Saturday, I was still a little shaken by what had happened at the bus stop. Had my instincts been right, or was I just being paranoid? I decided to shake it off and listen to some music in my bedroom before even looking at my homework. I kicked off my worn sneakers and cranked up the tunes. I started to dance. There was no one to see me make a fool out of myself, so why not? Besides, I love to dance. I kept time with the beat, moving my hips to the music.

Suddenly it came again. The strange feeling that I was being watched. Oh no. From behind me, someone laughed. I jumped nearly three feet off the ground. Slowly I turned to face the source of laughter.

There, on the windowsill looking comfortable and amused, sat Dustin. I stared at him with wide eyes, utterly speechless.

He smirked. "Don't stop on my account. You're an awesome dancer."

I felt my face get hot. He had seen me dance. However, that wasn't the big issue at the moment.

"H-how did you get in here?" I was finally able to stammer, after a full minute of simply staring in bewilderment.

Dustin shrugged. "It was easy. You really shouldn't leave your window open."

Excuse me? I was sure the window had been closed, and I told him so. Again I received a nonchalant shrug, which was beginning to seriously tick me off. The pity I had been feeling for him the day before was gone. All I felt now was annoyance that was quickly turning into anger.

"What are you doing here?" I asked as calmly as I could. My fingers curled into tight fists behind my back. If he shrugged again, I was sure I would slug him.

"I was bored, so I decided to come over to see what you were doing." He paused to tilt his head and smile. "I'm glad I did."

That beatific grin wasn't going to distract me. Not this time. "And how did you get up here?" I raised an eyebrow. "You're not some kind of vampire or anything freaky like that, are you? 'Cause I really do not need you bringing the whole Cullen clan into my bedroom."

"Nope. Completely human, I promise."

"In that case, you could have rung the doorbell like a normal human being."

"Yeah, but where's the fun in that?" he countered.

"How did you even get my address?"

"You gave it to me."

I glared at him. This boy was impossible. First he

breaks into my room and now he was insisting that I gave him my address. Which I totally didn't. Though something distracted me from being angry with him. If he could just appear on my windowsill, who's to say he couldn't follow me without my knowing? Maybe there had been someone there the other day. Maybe it was him. I stared at him, incredulous.

"What?" he demanded.

I mimicked his annoying shrug. "Nothing."

He cocked his head, trying to figure me out. "You know, you're kind of weird."

This brought the anger back. "*I'm* weird? I'm not the one sneaking into people's rooms. I should be calling the police right now, or at least telling my mom that you're here." I was so mad, my whole body had started to lightly shake.

Dustin just stared at me like a parent waiting for their child to get tired of having a temper tantrum. "But you're not going to," he told me calmly.

"Oh yeah? And how do you know that?" I snapped.

"I know you," he said simply.

What? That was a laugh. "Oh, please. You barely know me. It's been what? A few weeks?"

He didn't answer. He just stared at me with a smugness that made me want to scream.

I plopped down on my bed with my arms crossed, glowering at him. The staring contest went on for several seconds. Neither of us blinked.

"So when are you going to leave?" I asked finally.

Dustin leaned against the windowpane. "When you want me to."

"I want you to."

He shook his head. "No, you don't."

"Ugh! You are insufferable!" I exclaimed.

I was so frustrated my head would surely explode if I didn't calm down soon. His eyes gleamed with amusement. He was totally enjoying pushing my buttons.

"Couldn't you have picked some other girl to bother?"

He shrugged. "I'm interested in you."

Oh, good grief! Where had he gotten that line?

"Fine, you win. I give up. Stay as long as you want. I'm going downstairs for something to eat anyway. Have fun by yourself," I told him, heading for the door.

Dustin's facial expression turned from amusement to disappointment. He actually pouted. "Aw, come on, Lil. Don't be like that. If you want me to leave, I'll leave."

I froze. "Really?"

He nodded, beginning to maneuver so that he could climb down.

Then I realized that I didn't want him to go. This was the first time a boy had pursued me like this, and I was kind of flattered. Stupid, I know. Besides, he was my friend. He was annoying, not threatening.

"Dustin, wait. I can't believe I'm saying this, but you can stay if you want to. I'll get a snack for us, OK?"

He looked at me a little uncertainly. "OK." I don't think he trusted that I would really come back.

When I returned, I was half expecting him not to be there. Maybe I had dreamed the whole thing. But there he was, sitting in the same exact position. He was staring intently out the window, his expression sad.

"I'm back. As promised."

He looked up, all sadness erased. A wide grin spread across his face. How did he do that? Completely change his facial expressions in an instant, leaving me to think that maybe I had imagined his sadness. I tossed him a bag of pretzels as I sat down. He opened it, immediately beginning to munch.

This whole time, the music had been playing. I considered turning it off, but decided to keep it on. Why not?

Dustin finished the bag in record time. I tossed him another one. My aim was off. It went flying for the open window. However, he caught it out of midair without even blinking. Whoa.

"Nice reflexes," I commented, impressed.

"Thanks."

He opened the new bag and popped a pretzel in his mouth.

"So, what's your story?" he asked after eating a few more.

"Come again?" I asked, eyebrows furrowed.

"Well, I told you stuff about myself, so now it's your turn," he explained.

I sighed, figuring it was only fair. "Well, my mom is a secretary at the *Times Herald Record* newspaper. My dad fixes computers. Not very interesting jobs. Trust me. I've visited both." I pretended to yawn, emphasizing how boring they were.

Dustin laughed. "Any brothers or sisters?"

"Two brothers and one sister. I'm the oldest. Aaron's seven, Eric's five, and Rose is eleven."

"Wow. Big family," he commented.

I nodded. That was true, although I had seen bigger. My friend Asialie has five brothers and sisters. Whenever I go to her house, there's always shouting and the sound of something crashing to the floor.

There was silence, except for the music. I guessed that Dustin had either run out of questions or got tired of hearing about my dull life. Who could blame him? I was an ordinary girl with an ordinary life. On the other hand, just the fact that he was sitting on my windowsill showed that he wasn't just your average Joe.

My fingers eventually started thrumming on my knee to the beat. Soon my whole body was moving a little. Of course, I didn't dance, since Dustin was sitting right there, making me feel even more self-conscious than usual.

Dustin picked up on this. "You have to show me some of those moves you were doing when I came in."

I shook my head. No way. He had already seen enough. I wasn't going to make a total fool of myself with him right there to laugh at me.

"Please, please, please," he whined. "Look, I don't even know how to dance."

He abruptly stood up and started to dance. Or at least he tried to. He sort of flopped his arms around and moved his hips in the most awkward way I had ever seen. He kind of looked like he had to go to the bathroom. I watched in horror as he continued on to do the Cabbage Patch and the Shopping Cart. It was the last straw when he attempted—emphasis on attempted—to do the Chicken Noodle Soup.

"Fine, I give up! I'll show you some of my dance moves. I can't promise anything, though. I'm not exactly a trained dancer."

He rolled his eyes. "Does it look like I care? Just come on already!"

He grabbed my hand, pulling me to my feet. "Lay it on me."

I danced a little. He observed, then tried to mimic what I had just done. We did this over and over again, almost like a real dance lesson. He tripped a lot. I found it odd that he could climb up the side of my house and in through my window, quiet as a cat—or a cat burglar. Yet he was so clumsy with something as easy as dancing.

When he finally got a combination down, I wanted to laugh so badly, I thought I was going to burst. On the last part, he tripped and grabbed my arm. He ended up pulling me down with him.

He asked if I was all right. I tried to answer, but I couldn't stop laughing.

"Hey, what's so funny?"

"You're a terrible dancer," I gasped through a fit of giggles.

He pretended to be mad. " Oh, really?"

I continued to laugh uncontrollably. Then he began to tickle me. Oh no. I laughed even harder, grabbing a pillow and whacking him with it. Dustin fell back with an "Oof!" This time it was his turn to start laughing.

We didn't stop for a few minutes. Finally, Dustin helped me up. I turned the music off.

"Guess I should go now. Dad's gonna be wondering where I am."

"OK. See you later."

He climbed out the window. Then he leaned back in. "I had fun. Maybe I'll come back sometime."

He gave me a big smile. I smiled back. Then he was gone. My smile faded. I couldn't believe that I had let him into my bedroom. Sighing at my stupidity, I went downstairs.

That night, as I lay in bed, I thought about the surprise visitor I had found on my windowsill. My thoughts lingered on the way he had been staring out the window. It was almost like he was wishing for something. Something that he knew was impossible to wish for. Maybe he had been thinking about his mom. Then I began to wonder if he would climb in through my window again. I realized that I wanted him to. This both frightened and confused me. I decided to sleep on it.

THE PHONE CALL

The days passed quickly and, in a snap, the day of the Harvest Dance had arrived. Everyone was excited. The Harvest Dance was a costume party and one of the biggest dances of the whole entire school year. Only eighth graders were allowed to go, so we were psyched. My friends and I had been waiting for this since fifth grade.

The sixth and seventh graders were the only ones unhappy. They had to wait a whole year—or two—before they could go. Tough break. So, while most people chattered happily, they moped around the school. Some even looked kind of angry. To them, October was one of the worst months of the year.

My friends and I arrived at the party ten minutes after it started. Asialie and I had been over at Malerie's house an hour before to get ready. My grandmother, a well-known seamstress, had sewn us the most awesome costumes. I helped with the designs, of course. I have to say, my friends and I were knockouts.

Once we had entered the gym, our jaws all dropped at the same time. There were giant spiderwebs and orange and black balloons. Freakishly large spiders crawled up the walls.

The lights had been dimmed, casting a creepy shadow across the whole room. Jack-o-lanterns along with a huge disco ball hung from the ceiling. A big group of people stood and occasionally danced around the DJ booth.

I scanned the room for people I knew. It took some doing to recognize anyone. But soon I spotted Louis.

"Hey, you!" I hollered as I made my way toward him.

He turned to see who had called him. Fangs protruded from his mouth. His hair been gelled back. He wore a long black cape with the collar popped. His features were paler than usual. Spray-on blood trickled down the sides of his mouth. Classic vampire.

"Lily," he said slowly. "Wow, you look awesome."

I smiled. Well, I couldn't argue with him there. I had decided to dress up as a Gothic princess. My dress was made of black silk, the waist woven with faux maroon lilies. Black lace made up the sleeves, which came down to my elbows. The neckline was perfect. Not too low and not too high. Though black was the main color, slits in the fabric showed lavender underneath. The skirt billowed out from below the waist. It went all the way down to the floor.

I wore black eyeliner and mascara, my eye shadow a glittery purple. My cheeks shone dark red, and my lips were blood red and glossy. To top it off, my thick curly black hair was pulled up into a tight bun, crowned with a headband of black withered lilies.

I had just begun to compliment him on his own attire when Mal and Asialie came over. Louis's face suddenly turned kind of red. His eyes were on Malerie. "Whoa."

She stunned in a skillfully frayed baby blue prom dress. Her mother had really worked wonders with her makeup, making it look like the blood had been drained from her body. Dark shimmering circles under her eyes contrasted beautifully with her pale skin. A corsage of withered flowers had been wrapped around her wrist. A knife covered in blood stuck out of her side as if someone had just stabbed her.

The undead Prom Queen blushed. "You don't look so bad yourself."

Asialie, the Egyptian goddess, saw one of her friends and took off. My two remaining friends continued to stare at each other. I cleared my throat.

"I'm going to get some punch. Anybody want some?"

They seemed to have not heard me. I rolled my eyes and started for the snack table. As I crossed the room, I found very little breathing space, due to the dancing eighth graders.

The very second I went outside to get some air, someone's hands covered my eyes.

"You look great," a voice whispered in my ear.

I whirled around and caught my breath when I saw who was standing in front of me. The Phantom of the Opera. His black cape, white gloves, and half mask made him look sinister, maybe even dangerous. In the play, he's supposed to be ugly, but this one was the cutest phantom I had ever seen.

He grinned and took off his mask.

"Dustin," I gasped. "You nearly gave me a heart attack!"

He laughed. "Sorry about that, but I couldn't resist."

I playfully punched his arm. "Yeah, well, you got me."

He cocked his head. "Hey, why aren't you inside?"

I shrugged.

"Well, come on!"

He put the mask back on and pulled me back into the gym.

When we entered the room, the party was in full swing, pop music assaulting our ears. I dragged Dustin on the dance floor with me, evaluating his improvements. Thanks to me, he had gotten slightly better, but he occasionally still looked like he had to go to the bathroom.

At some point he took a break, claiming that he wanted to get a drink. I let him leave, pitying the boy for his sorry dancing skills. I assumed he simply wanted to avoid any further embarrassment. So I continued to dance with the rest of my friends while he slipped through the crowd. So far, the night had been everything I'd hoped for. Everything we'd pictured since fifth grade, and more.

Dustin did not reappear. By the time we all decided to get a drink at the snack table, nearly twenty minutes had gone by since I'd last seen him. I searched the crowd in puzzlement, wondering where he could have gone.

As if on cue, a flash of a black cape and dark curly hair caught my eye. I spotted Dustin sneaking out the back door. Where had he been all this time?

The minute I opened the door, a gust of air hit my face. With a slight shiver, I tugged my thin sweater tighter around me. Dustin stood with his back to me. His shoulders were tense and he held something sleek, shiny, and blue to his ear.

A cell phone.

"I'm not ready yet," I heard him say. "Just give me more time and I swear I won't let you down."

I stood completely still, not even taking a breath.

He sighed as if the weight of the world was on his shoulders. "Yes, I understand. I know what I'm doing. Just give me a few more weeks. Please."

He stopped talking to listen to whoever was on the other line. From the way he flinched a little, I could guess that the person had some harsh words to say in return. I could hear them yelling from where I stood.

"That won't be necessary," Dustin said quickly, voice strained. "I-I have to go. Lily and the others will come looking for me. See you later."

I jumped at the sound of my name. So he had told this person about me. Another sudden gust of wind pulled at my hair. My headband went sliding to the ground. Dustin whirled around, but by then I had escaped back into the gym, running at full speed. I didn't stop running until I was safely submerged into the big blob of people in the middle of the dance floor.

A few minutes after I had found my friends, Dustin approached, cool as a cucumber. He began chatting with Louis as if nothing had happened. So I turned to Malerie and did the same. I avoided him for the rest of the night. Whenever he tried to pull me aside to talk to me, I made up an excuse like having to go to the bathroom or complaining about how cold it would be outside. He soon got the hint and left me alone.

By the end of the dance I was a mess. I couldn't help but wonder who he was talking to and what they could possibly be talking about. I wanted to ask Dustin, but I was afraid he would accuse me of eavesdropping. Then what would I say?

When he approached me again as the cars rolled up to the curb, I opened my mouth to make another excuse. Then panicked when I realized that I couldn't think of one.

"I've been trying to give you this all night." Dustin handed me something withered and black. My headband. "You must have left it on the bench or something. I found it on the ground."

"Oh. Thanks." I swallowed.

"Lily," he started. "Did you—?"

Someone honked their car horn. Asialie beckoned for me to hurry up. Her mom was giving me a ride home.

"Time to go. Bye!" I hollered, already turning to leave. Feeling kind of bad for treating Dustin like that, I looked back. "Call you later. 'K?"

He nodded, confusion plain on his face. I turned away to hop in the car. I forced myself not to look back, knowing that if I did I would see him staring after me.

As I sat in the back seat of that car, only half listening to my friend's chatter, a sudden thought sent me shivering. Whatever this person wanted Dustin to do couldn't be good. And I had a horrible feeling that it had something to do with me.

ONE MESSED-UP
CHRISTMAS PRESENT

December rolled in and with it came winter break, which we were all looking forward to. Everyone was excited. Well, everyone except Dustin. He seemed to become more distant as the temperature dropped. The visits to my window stopped. I first assumed it was because of the snow and all, but I began to think that maybe this wasn't the case. Something was definitely eating at him. And no matter how hard I tried to get it out of him, he acted like he had no idea what I was talking about. I knew it had something to do with what I had overheard at the dance, but I wasn't exactly sure how to bring that up.

When the last day before winter break arrived, he was as quiet as ever. Even my friends had begun to notice the change. Frankly, the whole thing had me really annoyed, and I decided to make it my mission to cheer him up by the end of the day.

I was trying to figure out how to open my locker, since it was pretty much jammed with the amount of crap I had shoved in there the period before, when I spotted Dustin moping down the hallway with his head drooping. Uh-oh. I called his name, but he must not have heard me, because he kept on walking. I decided to go up to him.

I reached out to touch his shoulder. Before my hand could come in contact, he turned around. His expression was dark.

"Hey," I said cheerfully.

"Hello." He sounded kind of distracted.

I started to ask him what was wrong, already expecting the reaction before he cut me off.

"Oh. I was just looking for you. I have something to give you."

I flashed him a quizzical smile. "Really? What is it?"

"Well, since I won't see you during winter break, I thought I'd better give you your present," he said, pulling a rectangular box out of his pocket. He didn't open it, but instead just stared at it. The bell rang. He frowned and slipped it back into his pocket. "Guess I'll show you later."

"OK," I said, a little disappointed. I was itching to see what it was.

However, I had to get to class. Even though most of the teachers had decided not to even bother with any real classes, my math teacher had not been so lenient. And she would kill me if I arrived late. We quickly headed to class side by side without another word spoken.

Lunch came around and Dustin still didn't give me his present. I tried not to be bothered by it. He would give it to me soon enough. My friends had decided to hold our gift exchange at the lunch table. I had gotten them all gift cards, which they really appreciated.

31

Turns out my friends had all pitched in to give me one big present. It sat in the middle of the table. Sitting there was a big fluffy purple teddy bear holding a pink mini pillow. The word *Lily* had been embroidered onto the pillow. Flowers encircled my name. This had to be one of the cutest presents I had ever gotten. I could not stop grinning.

We continued to talk about our winter plans while unwrapping little presents. Instead of joining in on the fun, Dustin sat to the side, not talking to anyone. I tried to include him in the conversation, but he didn't respond.

The rest of the day somehow ended, and I got home to an empty house. My little sister Rose and the boys came home an hour later than I did. My parents were still at work and wouldn't be home until well after dark. So I had a whole hour to myself. Since we had a week off, I didn't even look at my homework. I retired to my room with a good book, plopped down on my bed, and began to read.

I was only about a chapter in when I heard a soft knocking on my window. With a sigh, I put the book down and opened my window wide enough for a person to crawl through. Dustin came inside, shivering from the bitter cold.

From the looks of it, he had been out there quite a while. Flakes of snow sparkled in his wet hair. A few had even been caught in his eyelashes. He wore a heavy winter coat and gloves that had to have cost hundreds of dollars. The idiot wore no hat or earmuffs, leaving his exposed ears to freeze until they were bright red.

"Are you insane?!" I hissed, hurriedly shutting the window behind him. "You could have frozen to death!"

He shook his head. "I'm stronger than you give me credit for. I'm sorry to bother you, but I need to give you my present."

He stepped forward and pulled out a familiar rectangular box. With shaking hands, he handed it to me.

I looked down at it, suddenly afraid to see what was inside.

"Open it," he whispered.

Slowly, I opened it. Gasping, I almost dropped the box. I gingerly took out the beautiful diamond necklace. A golden pendent dangled from the middle. It looked familiar somehow. Where had I seen this exotic piece of jewelry before? Recognition flooded my memory and my eyes grew wide. That picture. The necklace had been his mother's.

"Dustin, this is your—"

"Mom's," he finished for me. "I know."

I put it back in the box and handed it back to him, shaking my head. "I can't take this. It's way too valuable to give to me. Why would you give me something like this, anyway?"

He refused to take it back. "No. I want you to have it. The necklace will look great on you. Besides, there's plenty more where that came from."

"But what about your dad? Didn't he give this to her?" I asked.

He shrugged. "He said it was OK that I give it to you."

I cast my eyes down. "I-I don't know what to say."

Dustin closed my fingers around the box with his warm gloved hands. "Then don't say anything. Just take it as a Christmas present from my dad and me. Here, put it on."

With a slight frown, I opened the box again. Dustin helped secure it around my neck. We looked at each other in the mirror. His mother's jewelry glistened and sparkled against my neck. I had never ever received something as beautiful and expensive as this.

"See, I told you it'd look great on you," he commented quietly.

Why was he giving me this? Yes, I felt honored that he'd done it, but that didn't stop me from feeling guilty.

Dustin took a step back. "Guess I should be going now."

"If you ever want this, just ask and I'll return it," I told him honestly.

The ends of his mouth twitched up into a little smile. "Thanks. You know, you're a good friend."

"I know how much she meant to you."

The smile faltered. He seemed to be contemplating something. He took a step closer. I stared at him, wondering what he was doing.

He took a deep breath. "I haven't been telling you the whole truth. I'm not . . . I'm not who you think I am."

His eyes did not meet mine. Dustin reached out to touch the sparkling horse pendent that rested on my collarbone. I stood very still, anxious to know what he was about to tell me. He didn't say anything else; he continued to study the golden horse. As he flipped it over, I noticed something on the back. It was a small computer chip of some kind. A tiny green light flashed.

Dustin must have noticed it too, because he stiffened, eyes locked on the flashing green light. He muttered a curse under his breath.

"I'm out of time," he whispered, talking more to himself than to me.

Without warning, he ripped the necklace from my neck, threw it down on the floor, and stomped on it with all his might.

I gave him a hard shove. "Hey, what do you think you're doing?"

"The necklace had to be destroyed."

"But it was your mom's," I protested.

He sighed. "The necklace is a tracking device. We met for a reason, Lily."

I stared at him. He must have been joking. This was a joke, right? But he was dead serious.

I turned away. "You're crazy."

He grabbed my hand. "Come with me. Please. You gotta believe me. Your family could be in danger!"

My eyes flicked between his hand holding mine and the urgent expression on his face. His eyes were pleading and full of regret. He seemed completely spooked. Should I trust him? If my family was in danger, then I had to.

"Fine," I said. "But only for a minute."

He sighed with relief. "Come on." He opened the window wide.

How were we supposed to get down? But Dustin was already ahead of me. He took a silver trinket out of his pocket. He pressed a button and threw it onto the ground below. There was a soft popping sound. Then, slowly, a metal ladder began to materialize out of nowhere right in front of my eyes. I couldn't believe what I was seeing. It was impossible.

Dustin hurriedly made a beeline for the ladder. I followed him down, trying very hard to ignore the height. Dustin helped me down the last few rungs. He pressed the button again. The ladder folded into itself about a gazillion times before turning into a shiny little trinket again. He picked it up and stuffed it back in his pocket.

I glanced up at the sky, which had faded to an ugly gray. The snow had begun to fall even harder. I had to blink several times in order to see three feet in front of me. The wind was picking up, throwing around my hair this way and that, making it even tougher to see. I was absolutely freezing, because I only wore a sweater. If Dustin hadn't gone into complete freak mode, I would have taken the time to grab a coat or something warm.

He took a firm hold of my hand and raced down the street. I tried to keep up, but he was going too fast. He had longer legs than I did. So I stumbled along behind him, begging him to slow down. However, he didn't appear to be listening. He just kept muttering something about needing more time.

Finally we reached town. The whole place was completely deserted. No one wanted to be outside in this weather.

Neither did I. I longed to be in my nice warm room again and mentally kicked myself for getting into this mess.

I stopped short, demanding that we take a break. Dustin argued that we didn't have time to stop, but eventually relented. We took refuge on the stoop of one of the closed shops. I shivered violently from the cold. I couldn't feel my fingers or my cheeks. My whole body felt completely frozen.

Dustin glanced over at me. I glared at him, hugging myself in a sad attempt to keep warm. He started to take his coat off. I opened my mouth to stop him, but my teeth were chattering too much. He removed his coat and draped it around my shoulders. He also took off his gloves, slipping them onto my frozen hands.

I shook my head, working hard to get a sentence out.

"Y-you're g-gonna get s-sick."

Dustin laughed quietly, as if afraid someone would hear.

"I've s-suffered colder t-temperatures than this."

I frowned. "When?"

Before he could answer, there was a crack of twigs. Both of our heads turned at the noise. We jumped off the stoop, breaking into a full-out sprint.

Out of nowhere, something came up from behind me and yanked me back. I tried to scream, but a cloth had been put over my mouth. My attempted screams came out muffled, inaudible. I kicked and struggled, but my captor seemed to be made of steel. His iron grasp didn't loosen an inch, even when I kicked him where it counted.

I looked around for Dustin, wondering if he was in the same predicament. He stood a few yards away, arguing with a suited man. The man's face was grim. Even in the dim light of dusk, I could see the angry scar on the side of his face. It made him look even scarier. This guy was obviously much bigger than my friend, but Dustin appeared to have the power.

I heard the burly man say, "Yes, sir. I'll tell him. Please calm down. Your father wished to make the move tonight. Take it up with him. These are just my orders."

They turned toward me. When our eyes met, my so-called friend turned away. The scary guy gave a short nod to the guy holding me. His hold on me immediately loosened. But it wasn't enough for me to get away.

About a second later, I felt a sharp stinging on my arm. I cried out in pain and surprise. My eyesight became really blurry. I felt like I was sinking underwater. My legs turned to jelly, and my head suddenly became too heavy for me to hold up. In a matter of seconds, my feet slipped out from under me. Everything began to spin. Sounds became very far away and distant. I was drowning. Breathing turned into a laborious task. I gasped for air, desperate to breathe. Something pressed against my chest and wouldn't get off. I was hot and cold at the same time. Spots appeared in front of my eyes. I thought I heard the distant sound of a school bus. I wouldn't be home to get the kids off the bus. Mom was going to kill me.

The last thing I remember before passing out was the strong grip on my arms, which strangely comforted me. At least it let me know that I wasn't really falling. I saw red. Then black. After that, POW! I was out like a light.

QUESTIONS

I was running through the forest, trying to get away from whoever was following me. It was pitch black except for the moonlight. Shadows surrounded me, lurking behind every shrub. Trees reached out to pull me into a bone-crushing hug with their ragged branches. The howls of coyotes and other ravenous animals were carried to my ears by the wind.

Besides that, it was silent. Eerily silent. Somehow I knew finding Dustin would be the only way out of here. I frantically searched for some kind of opening. Thorns scratched at my face and legs. My knees stung from scrapes and bruises. Every bone in my body ached.

I heard what sounded like the roar of a motor. I ran toward it, tripping along. The roar stopped, leaving the forest quiet again. First I shook with anger. Then I fell to the ground, not bothering to get up. I would be stuck in here forever.

Something clamped around my waist, forcing me up. It pulled and pulled, dragging me into the depths of the forest. I fought it in vain. The thing was on a mission. So I let it drag me, too weak to fight anymore.

I woke up with a start. Within seconds, I remembered everything. Groggily rubbing the sleep out of my eyes, I searched for my glasses. They were on the nightstand next to me.

Once I had slipped them on, I glanced around. I was in a bedroom, but it was far from the hostile environment I'd expected. The walls were a lovely teal color and decorated with landscape paintings. On the wall beside me was an open window. The bright sun warmed my face. I got up and wobbled toward it, feeling light-headed. I reached out the window. My fingers were stopped by what felt like bars, but I couldn't see anything but the snowy landscape beyond. Slowly, I reached out to touch the window again. Yep. They were there. How could that be? They would have to have been invisible.

Shaken, I plopped back down on my bed. This was all Dustin's fault. It was my fault too. I had been dumb enough to trust him. To think he was my friend. To let him climb through my window. And finally, the icing on the cake, to very stupidly allow him to lead me away from my home. I felt like kicking something.

Hot tears ran down my cheeks. Now I had no idea what was going to become of me. Whoever these people were, why did they want me? How quickly would my parents miss me? Would there be a trail for the police to follow? Would someone put two and two together and figure out what happened?

Oh, jeez. My head hurt like crazy. Then I noticed the bear holding the embroidered pillow sitting at the end of the bed. How did that get there? It had been in my bedroom. Had the kidnappers been back in my house?

A few minutes later, the door opened. A woman who appeared to have stepped right out of a movie from the fifties entered the room.

She smiled warmly. "I see that you're finally awake. How are you feeling?"

I gave her a look. "Just awesome." I knew it was rude to be sarcastic, but seriously. I had just been kidnapped and now I was being held prisoner in a strange room. How did she think I was feeling?

She placed her cool hands on my forehead. I noticed a nametag on her shirt that read *Doreen*. "You must be hungry. I'll be back in a jiffy."

Before I could say anything, she had bustled away.

She had said "finally awake." I wondered how long I had been out. Everyone had to be looking for me now. Would they find me in time? Before . . . The truth is, I honestly had no idea what was going to happen to me.

True to her word, Doreen came back just moments later, carrying a tray with tea and a cheese sandwich. She set it down on the table beside me and just stood there with her hands on her hips. I looked up at her, confused. She stared pointedly at the tray, then at me. Finally understanding what she wanted, I took a bite of the sandwich and a sip of the tea. It warmed up the whole inside of my chest. Already my headache didn't feel so bad.

When I was done, Doreen picked up the tray and turned to leave.

"Doreen," I called.

"Yes, Miss Mason?"

"Something bad is going to happen to me, isn't it?" My voice sounded shakier than I meant for it to sound.

Her expression softened. "Don't you worry. Nothing bad is going to happen to you."

I sat back in bed. "If you say so."

She smiled and was gone, leaving me alone in the teal room once again.

A few minutes later, I got up and tried the door, just to see what would happen. Locked from the outside, of course.

I went into the bathroom and took a look in the mirror. With heavy bags under my bloodshot eyes, chapped lips, and frizzy hair going in every direction, I looked simply horrible. First, I turned on the sink faucets and flung water in my face. Then I stretched and slapped my cheeks around a bit. I brushed and tied my hair back with a scrunchy as best as I could.

After taking a long shower, I was feeling as refreshed as a girl being held against her will can feel. Walking out with a towel wrapped around me, I discovered that a pile of brand new clothes and underwear had been neatly placed on the bed. There was also a bag full of toiletries. I uncapped the toothpaste, took out my new toothbrush, and scrubbed my teeth until they hurt. Then I slowly got dressed. The weird part? Everything fit me perfectly. Talk about creepy.

Once done with sprucing myself up, I searched the room for any way to escape. No such luck. I did find some books, though. That was something to keep me occupied at least. I picked a random one, took a seat on the plush carpet, and began reading.

There was a soft knock on the door. Not even bothering to look up from the very interesting book, I told whoever it was to come in. The person quietly entered. Figuring that it was probably just Doreen, I still didn't look up.

My visitor cleared his throat. "Hello, Lily."

I jumped, sending the book flying out of my hands. A cold chill went down my spine and a rush of anger made my hands shake. The memory of last night, of being tricked and captured, all came flooding back. I kept my head down, picked up the book, and pretended to continue reading. Maybe if I just didn't acknowledge him, he would march right back through that door and never come back.

"Could you please look at me?" he begged.

It became clear that he wasn't going anywhere. Forced to address him, I told him to go away through very tightly clenched teeth. He still didn't move.

"Don't be like that. Just let me explain."

Explain? He must be joking. No explaining was ever going to get me to forgive him, and he knew that. My head snapped up and I glowered at him like I've never glowered at anybody before. The anger that I felt toward him was so strong, I could hardly contain it. He must have realized this, because he was backing up, quickly.

"Don't you want to know what's going on?" he asked, hands in the air like he was about to get arrested or something.

I stood up and advanced toward him. "What I want to

know is how I could have been so stupid to trust you. Part of me knew something was off about you from the minute I met you. The way you were looking at me. It was just weird. Why would a cute rich guy like you be interested in a girl like me? It made no sense."

Dustin stopped backing up and let his hands fall to his sides. "You have to understand, I wasn't acting. You were all really my friends. You're the only one I ever told about my mom. No one else."

I wasn't buying it. Not anymore. "Save it for someone who cares, Dustin. Real friends don't trick their friends and lie to them from the start. The only reason you approached me that day was because you had to. That whole 'I'm having a bad day too' stuff, that was just an act. You wanted me to feel bad and second-guess myself. Admit it."

Knowing that I was right, he didn't answer.

After a long, uncomfortable pause, he said, "All that doesn't matter now. What matters is that you're here now and we need to talk."

I didn't really hear anything past "All that doesn't matter." It sure as heck did matter. The traitor had lured me away from everything that I ever cared about. My family. My friends. My life. All gone because of him, and my foolishness. There was no telling what these people wanted from me—and I was certain they had no intention of letting me go. So yes, it mattered a lot.

Now, I'm the kind of person that doesn't get into fights. "Goody Two-Shoes" is what my friends call me sometimes.

However, at this moment, I was too furious to be my old self. Before he could finish talking, I pounced.

We tumbled to the ground. He must have been taken by surprise, because I got one punch in before he started fighting back. Unfortunately, he was a lot stronger than I was and had me pinned in a matter of minutes. With a scream of rage, I kicked and squirmed. I even bit him. He flinched, but didn't loosen his grip.

"Get off of me!" I shrieked.

"Not until you promise to listen. Look, I know you're angry and I don't blame you, but please. I need to explain."

I quit struggling and glared at him. "Fine, but so far, listening to you has only caused me trouble."

He nodded, letting me go.

I jumped up and turned my back on him, slowly walking over and taking a seat at the edge of my bed. The good-for-nothing liar sat down next to me.

Running a hand through his hair, he said with a sigh, "Well, I guess I should start with telling you where we are. The truth is, I'm not exactly sure about that one myself. We're somewhere in Pennsylvania. This much I know. I've never been to this particular branch before. All I know is, it's close enough for me to still attend school—"

"Whoa, hold up," I interrupted. "You're still going to school? Our school? Kindred Valley?"

He nodded slowly. "A helicopter took me to my old house this morning. If both of us disappeared at the same time, people would get suspicious, don't you think? But I'm transfering out, as of tomorrow. Anyway, may I go on?"

I crossed my arms. "Please."

Dustin cleared his throat. "Well, umm . . . soon after my mother died, my dad quit his job. Refused to speak to anyone. Even me. But then, one day he came up with this big idea. He wouldn't say what it was exactly. Just that it would change the world and make it a better place. He started calling in favors and that's how this organization began. C.I.A.T., Children In Attentive Training. Schools and camps started to pop up all over the place, teaching kids within the age range of five to seventeen how to do everything, be everything. I had never seen anything like it.

"Of course, I started attending one of his schools right away. And I did live in Florida. That much is true. And not to brag or anything, but now I can do anything. Pick locks, use various types of guns, drive a car, even construct one. You name it. However, there's one thing that separates me from the rest of the students. Apparently I'm a smooth talker. I can make anyone do just about anything I want. So that's why I'm what my dad calls the Recruiter. I persuade kids to leave their homes and come join us. Sometimes Dad gets a little impatient, though."

He paused, glancing at me. "Heard enough?"

I shook my head. "Not in the least. Go on."

Dustin sighed, going on to tell me that I was his biggest challenge. The first girl his age that he ever had to recruit. He had been given orders to gain my trust and persuade me to come join him, like usual. If that didn't work, he'd have had to force me. According to him, something changed. He wasn't counting on liking me or making any friends. The time that he spent with me and the others had been the most fun he had since his mom died.

"That's why you have to believe me," he continued. "I never wanted to trick you. I was just . . . doing my job. My dad's tactics aren't the greatest. Sometimes in order to pass their exams, the students have to do things that aren't exactly legal."

Dustin looked away. "I was supposed to take you sooner, but I got stupid and took my time. Then, when he gave me that necklace, I knew what his intentions were. I got paranoid and tried to get you as far away as possible, but they found us. I'm so sorry, Lily, but whatever he has planned has to be something good. He said so himself."

This sounded more like a question than a conviction to me. He finished talking and looked at me suspiciously, wondering why I was being so quiet. My mind whirled with all he had just told me. All this information was a lot to process all at once. He still stared at me, expecting me to say something.

"So you persuade people to come here, like, of their own free will? Does that mean I can leave if you haven't convinced me?"

He looked at the floor. "Like I said, you're . . . special."

"Then I guess we're done talking." I said, already turning away. "Can you leave?"

He just looked at me for a minute, a little taken aback. "Yes, I can leave if you want me to. Is that all you have to say? Any questions or anything?"

I just shook my head. He turned to leave.

"And Dustin," I called.

He froze, looking back at me over his shoulder. "Yeah?"

"Maybe you liked me a little back at home, but here we're not friends. I don't think we ever can be friends again. You only told me about your mom so that I'd feel sorry for you. It was all just one big game. I don't care what your excuse is, this whole idea of your dad's isn't normal. And if you had any kind of brain, you would know that. Believe whatever you want to believe, but just to make things absolutely clear, stay away from me."

For a second, Dustin looked hurt, but then his face smoothed into a cold, expressionless mask. "I'm supposed to give you a tour tomorrow and show you the ropes, so that's going to be kind of hard. I'm sorry that you feel that way, but if you don't want to be friends, then fine. That's just fine with me." His voice was like ice. He turned to leave, slamming the door behind him.

I threw the book at the door, wishing I could have hit his head with it. How dare he be angry with me just because I didn't want to be friends with him anymore? Of course I didn't. He had been lying to me the whole time about everything. He had been pretending to be my friend. With friendship comes trust, and I definitely did not trust him. It had all been part of his father's plans for his demented "organization." It sounded more like some kind of messed-up conspiracy to me. Although Dustin may not have wanted to admit it, he knew something wasn't right. Whatever. His dad was a loon and so was he.

Well, good riddance to the both of them! I had to find a way to get out of there.

I ran to the door and tugged at the brass doorknob. Still locked. Then I dashed to the window. The invisible bars were still there. I had no idea how to get out, so I went back to the bed and put my head in my hands. I decided to wait and check out my surroundings when Dustin gave me the tour. Maybe I could pretend to give him another chance and play him like he played me. Then I decided against it. I've never been a very good liar and I really didn't have the energy to try. I didn't want anything to do with that traitor anyway.

He made me feel like such an idiot. Of course I was kind of stupid for letting him get me kidnapped, but that's beside the point. To make things worse, now that I thought about it, part of me wanted to believe him. He had seemed so sincere when he tried to explain. Maybe he really was just a confused boy who thought he was working for the greater good. Not to mention those eyes. Those beautiful eyes of his boring into mine, begging me to understand. The thing is, I had thought of him as a really good friend. Yes, I was angry with him. Yes, I had told him that we weren't friends, but my brain was having a little trouble processing that along with all the other stuff swirling around in there.

He's not my friend. He's not my friend, I told myself over and over again, lying down on my comfy canopy bed. There was nothing to do but wait. I hated waiting, but that was what I had to do.

THE TOUR

My "tour guide" arrived the next afternoon. He entered cautiously, as if afraid I would attack him again.

"Don't worry. I'm not going to jump you or anything," I assured him, rolling my eyes and standing up.

Dustin's shoulders relaxed a bit, but not fully. I didn't blame him.

As he got closer, I noticed something. His left cheek looked a little bruised and there was an angry scarlet bite mark on his wrist.

"Did I do that?" I asked quietly, already knowing the answer.

He glanced down at where I was staring. He flashed me a sheepish grin. "Yeah."

I lowered my eyes, feeling ashamed. Just because I was mad at him didn't mean I had to attack him like that. He had only wanted to talk to me and I'd jumped him before he got the chance.

"I acted like a savage yesterday. Even if it is your fault that I'm here, I shouldn't have attacked you. I'm really, really sorry."

"Don't be," he said, surprised that I was showing remorse for my actions. "I deserved it."

We stared at the floor, neither of us that sure what to say to each other. Everything had already been said the day before.

Dustin coughed. "Umm, how about we start that tour?"

Eager to leave the somewhat suffocating room, I agreed. We stepped out into what appeared to be a dorm hallway. Identical doors lined both walls. Golden plaques with names on them had been placed on each door. I turned to see if a golden plaque was on my door with my name on it. There it was. Knowing how rich his father was, you could bet it was real gold.

I had always imagined seeing my name in shiny golden letters, but not like this. With the situation I was in, it didn't impress me as much as it would have. It saddened me instead. That plaque on the door implied that I would be stuck there for a long time. If not forever. It was a symbol of my freedom being ripped away from me, perhaps never to return.

Quickly I looked away and followed Dustin down the hall.

"So, this is where the captured kids stay," I commented.

He stopped for a second. "Many of them are not here against their will, you know."

I scowled. "You mean like me."

He pretended not to hear. He looked thoughtful for a minute and continued to walk. "Some of their parents are almost as rich as Dad. They heard of Dad's plan and wanted their kids to be a part of it. On the other hand, some of these kids came here from the streets. If they stay here, they get clothing, food, and shelter. All they have to do is work for him."

I was speechless. There really was nothing to say after that. What kind of parents would give up their kids like that? Did they even know what this so-called "plan" was?

We entered the lobby. The receptionist was just so thrilled to see us, she nearly hopped right out of her chair in excitement. Not.

"Whaddya want?" she asked, chewing her gum and reading a magazine. I swear, she was just like all the stereotypes.

"I'm signing out one of the occupants," Dustin said nonchalantly.

She eyed me, sizing me up. I guessed she didn't find anything particularly interesting about me, since her expression remained indifferent and bored. I stared right back at her—mostly because one of her fake eyelashes had begun to slide off. I wondered why she didn't just use mascara. I had a strong urge to pull it off myself, but decided against it.

Dustin finished signing me out and took my arm, gently pulling me along.

I yanked my arm out of his grasp. "Just how long am I going to be an 'occupant' here?"

He refused to meet my annoyed gaze. "I'm not exactly sure. Usually kids are let go when they turn eighteen. You might be a different story."

I folded my arms, glaring at him until he looked at me. "Oh, that's right. I'm special. What exactly does that mean, anyway?"

He shifted uncomfortably. "Like I said, you're the first girl that I brought here. My father said that he has certain plans for you."

"I'll bet you any amount of money that his plans have something to do with me becoming your girlfriend. Your partner in crime," I said flatly.

He looked away. "I dunno. Maybe."

Exasperated with him, I started trotting ahead of him, not caring if he followed me or not.

"Lily, wait," he called.

There was no need to call me, because I had already stopped in my tracks. I stared at the scene before me with my mouth wide open. We were standing on a balcony facing a mega huge room. The walls seemed to be made of metal. I could see everything from where we stood.

There was some kind of martial arts class going on in the south side of the room. In the meantime, kids of all ages were climbing a tall rock wall located on the west side. However, it wasn't a normal rock wall. Some of the rocks fell away once they had been touched. And was it me, or did the whole thing shake? This was definitely unlike any rock wall I had ever seen. A big obstacle course with hurdles, ladders, ropes, poles, and many other things had been set up in the middle of the room. Many of the boys did push-ups and sit-ups while the girls did rope climbing.

"This is one of the training facilities. Some are more fun than others."

I swept my eyes over the room. "What about the other facilities?"

"Come on and I'll show you." Dustin answered, leading me down the stairs and into the crowd.

About a billion eyes locked on me as we passed by. I stared down at the hard floor, hurrying to catch up with him.

"Cover your ears," he warned as he opened a big door.

Suspiciously I obeyed. We had stepped into a shooting range. There were rows and rows of slots to shoot in. Most of them were occupied.

"So this is how you learned to use a gun," I shouted over the noise.

"Yeah, I started learning at about eight. Didn't get the hang of it until a year later."

I shook my head in wonder.

We entered yet another room. A gym. Treadmills lined the walls, a mini flat screen on each. A basketball game was in session, guys versus girls. Dustin cut in to shoot some hoops.

I watched him laugh and goof off with the others. What really struck me was that they seemed happy. It was as if they were right where they wanted to be. I couldn't understand why they didn't stop and look around. They were being held prisoner. Sure, it was with their friends, and yeah, it was fun, but there was no escape. They couldn't leave even if they wanted to. Had they given up hope? Did the thought ever cross their minds? Maybe, like Dustin, they had been brainwashed into thinking they were all a part of something bigger and greater than them. Didn't anyone see that this was wrong?

My supposed tour guide finally got out of the sweaty group and joined me, breathing hard.

"Sorry about that," he apologized with a smile. "The rest of the tour is outside, so come on." Taking my hand, he led me through yet another door. Once we were out, I pulled my hand out of his.

We continued along a stone walkway through what looked like a park. The climate was slightly warmer here. Bare-limbed trees lined our path. Frost replaced snow. I removed my gloves, stuffing them into my pocket. Other kids were taking a short stroll as well, holding books and chatting with their friends. The real bookworms sat on benches, reading and catching up on homework. You'd think it was a normal day at a normal park.

As we rounded a corner, we came upon a totally different scene.

Some sort of boot camp was in full swing as we passed. The children looked strange in their camouflage outfits and big Timberland boots. A bulky man yelled and yelled at them until he was red in the face. Spittle as well as orders spewed from his big fat mouth. I wondered how he could possibly be so hard on them. Some couldn't have been older than six, just a year older than my youngest brother. My arms ached from just watching them do push-up after push-up without any sign of stopping. I could only imagine how grueling that must have felt. The thought that I would soon be there right alongside them made me shudder.

I looked up at Dustin, sudden anger blazing through my veins. "Your dad is a terrible man."

"It's not as bad as you think," he mumbled as some kind of weak excuse.

Staring down at the ground, I quickened my steps, forcing him to lag behind. I purposely turned my whole body away from the camp. My dumb tour guide sped up to catch up with me. Suddenly I was looking down at his shiny white sneakers. Not a speck of dirt on them. Did a maid, like, clean them with a toothbrush every day? More likely he had a new pair for each day.

"Look, I know it seems bad, but these guys were given time to practice and get into shape before they were allowed to go to boot camp, and so will you. Then you'll have a fitness test to be sure you're ready. Don't worry. I'll be there to help you train every step of the way," he assured me.

Was that supposed to make me feel better? Because it didn't. Not at all.

He touched me lightly on my shoulder. "Try to make it work. I mean, it's not like you have a choice. So why not make the best of it? Here you have access to all this great stuff. The food's awesome and you can pretty much learn anything you want."

I shrugged him off and glared at him, hands balled into fists. "You don't get it, do you? I don't care if this place has great stuff, and I *don't* want to make the best of it. I was doing just fine before I met you. So no, I don't need you or this funny farm. What I want is my life back. And since you're obviously not going to help me get it back, I'll have to find a way to do it on my own. This place means nothing to me. You hear me? NOTHING!"

By this time I was screaming, tears running down my cheeks. My vision was blurry, but I could see Dustin's shocked expression. I could feel the people staring, but I didn't care. Let them stare. I had bigger fish to fry.

Dustin began to say something, but I didn't hear, because I had already taken flight. Not in any particular direction either. I simply had to get away from him.

After a while I grew tired of running and dropped to the ground right where I was. Luckily, my feet had carried me to a clearing. So I lay down on the hard blanket of frozen grass and stared up at the sky. The sky was a light shade of blue and large white puffballs of clouds drifted by.

One cloud looked almost exactly like an ice cream cone. It reminded me of the time I had gone to Mr. Freeze with Ella. Some little kid dropped his ice cream cone on her brand new eighty-dollar boots. We bought him a new one and cleaned off her boots as best as we could. Ella complained about how her mom would kill her when she found out. I laughed the whole time.

Instead of making me sad, the memory made me smile. It hadn't happened that long ago. I could still taste the sweet mint chocolate chip. Mmm. My favorite. Mr. Freeze had the best ice cream ever. It was one of the biggest hangouts in all of Kindred Valley.

The quiet made me want to lie dozing forever. Then I wouldn't have to think about anything. Just live in the memories. I heard movement. My whole body tensed. So much for dozing. The intruder stood above me.

"There you are," he said, sounding relieved.

My eyes remained fixated on the clouds. "Why did you choose me?"

"Huh?" was his only response.

"Why me? Your father could have picked anyone he wanted, but he had to have me. Why?"

Dustin lay down beside me without being invited. "I'm not sure. He usually picks kids through hacking into school records. He checks out the highest grades. The teachers' comments. Stuff like that. Then, once he finds someone he likes, he sends me to check him out." I could hear the smile in his voice. He really was clueless.

"I ran away just now. But no guards hunted me down or anything. Why not?"

"The property is extensive," he said. "There's a . . . barrier you wouldn't have been able to cross. I would have stopped you before anything bad happened."

We both didn't say anything for a few minutes, lost in thought. I wondered if he would ever snap out of it and have any grasp of what was going on here. Didn't he ever question why they would need a barrier in the first place? And just what would have happened if I had found the barrier?

"You called me cute," Dustin said suddenly. Well, wasn't that completely out of the blue?

I turned my head to look at him. "Excuse me?"

"When we were in your room. You called me a cute rich guy," he explained, grinning like an idiot.

Was he nuts? "Why are you thinking about that now?"

He shrugged. "I dunno. It just popped into my head."

I pulled my glasses down my nose and gave him the annoyed-librarian look. "Just because I called you cute doesn't mean I like you. Anyway, I was talking about before I really knew you."

He flashed me a smile that put the sun to shame. "Admit it, though. You still think I'm cute."

I rolled my eyes. "As if you're totally unaware of your good looks. You are the most arrogant, trickiest twit of a boy I've ever met."

"That was cold," he said after a stunned pause.

"So was tricking me into being captured and brought here against my will. Kidnapping someone and transporting her across state lines is a felony for a reason!"

"You've got a point there."

There was yet another awkward silence between us. Winter birds chattered happily, not a care in the world. I wished that I could be like them. I wished I could just spread my wings and fly away. I never thought I'd see the day where I'd miss my rowdy brothers, but I did. I missed everyone.

Tears pooled up at the rims of my eyes and escaped down the sides of my cheeks. I was immediately angry with myself for crying. Bawling my eyes out wouldn't help anything. Too much of it had been going on with me lately and it needed to stop. To make matters worse, Dustin saw the tears.

"Hey, are you OK?"

I sat up and turned my back to him, furiously wiping away at my cheeks. No use. The waterworks kept on coming and wouldn't stop. Eventually I just let the tears fall. My whole body shook with the sobs that came from deep within my chest. A painful lump clogged my throat and I had to gasp the air in big gulps to breathe. I hugged myself in a useless attempt to stop the shaking.

Dustin moved closer. He awkwardly put an arm around my shoulders, trying to comfort me. I automatically leaned into him. At this moment I really did not care. He stiffened, like he wasn't sure what to do. Then he slowly relaxed and let me wet up his shirt. We sat like that for what felt like an eternity.

When my tears finally subsided, the sun was going down. I removed my glasses, wiped them on my shirt, and put them back on. I felt a little better.

My now-drenched tour guide looked me over warily. "Are you feeling any better?"

He really did sound concerned. Maybe I had been wrong about him.

"Yeah, I'm OK. Sorry for soaking you."

He smiled. "It's fine. At least now I don't have to take a shower."

I scooted away from him. "Gross!"

We both laughed a little.

Dustin stood up and stretched. "So, do you want to finish the tour or head back?"

I considered. "Finish the tour." I would need all the information I could get to plot my eventual escape—although I was still expecting the cavalry any day now.

He helped me up and we silently left the clearing. He had his arm draped around my shoulders again. There was no need, since I wasn't crying anymore. Rolling my eyes, I shrugged his arm off. Not unkindly, though. He just blushed and kept on walking.

We came across a hospital, which seemed odd.

"This is for if someone gets injured after a mission or during training," he explained.

I shook my head in disbelief. A whole hospital! There must have been a whole lot of injuries, then. A sudden shiver went down my back. What injuries did they have? Obviously it wasn't just cuts and bruises. Then there'd be no need for a hospital, and a big one at that. And what were these so-called missions? Would I be going on one?

Next we stopped at a very tall building. It had to have been at least five stories high.

"I don't think I was supposed to bring you here," Dustin murmured.

"Then why did you?"

As he shrugged at this question, we heard voices. He pulled me behind a bush. Two men and two women, all wearing starched white jackets, came into view. They appeared to be pushing something.

"Move over," I hissed. "I can't see a thing."

I gave him a little shove. I focused very hard on what they were pushing. It looked like a stretcher. Wait a second—I thought the hospital was in the other direction. A little girl was lying there. From where I was sitting, she appeared to be unconscious, her long brown hair dangling off one end of the stretcher. Her arms were folded across her chest. She was perfectly still. The only way I knew she wasn't dead was because of her rosy cheeks. The men opened the door to the tall building and the women wheeled her inside. The men looked back, as if making sure that nobody had seen. I ducked down. Then they closed the door behind them and all was silent.

"Dustin." I turned to face him. "Explain."

To my dismay, he seemed as confused as me. "I don't know, all right? Dad doesn't tell me everything. But I do have a theory." He paused and shook his head. "Never mind. It's probably nothing."

"Come on. You have to tell me."

He bit his bottom lip, unsure. I stared at him in that pleading way he always stared at me when he wanted something. He cracked. "OK."

Dustin told me his father was a scientist. Before his mother died, his dad used to do these experiments on stuff like how much intelligence you can cram into someone's brain before it all becomes too much. There was some kind of experimental steroid he had been working on to enhance your brain functions, but it was too dangerous to test on

63

anyone but rats. However, Dustin had an idea that since his father had access to all of these kids, he'd taken the liberty of experimenting on them.

Dustin looked straight into my eyes when he said, "I'm not really sure what's going on. I've seen some kids being led away by people in white coats like those people we just saw, pretending to be doctors, but I don't think they were. Some kids never even came back. The ones that did refused to talk about it. In a way, it was like they couldn't. It was really weird. Lily, I . . . I don't know what to do."

I stared at him, completely at a loss for words. Then we both turned our attention to the tall building that now seemed so sinister. A dark shadow loomed above it. I started to imagine the screams of innocent children. Quickly I gave myself a good shake, looking away. Dustin's "theory" was already getting to me.

He tugged at my sleeve. "Let's go. It's getting late. My father will be wondering where we are."

I willingly followed. A plan began to take shape in my head. Somehow I knew that I was going to get those kids out of there and shut that whole horrible place down. I just wasn't sure how yet.

NIGHTTIME RUN

That night, instead of lying in bed, I sifted through my new clothes for anything black. I eventually found a black turtleneck and pants. After quickly changing, I tried the door. It swung wide open. They trusted me too much. With a sly grin, I quietly slipped out of the room.

Although I didn't really have a plan, I did have an objective. Find a way out. There was always a loophole. I just had to find it. Then, once I was out, I could blow the whistle on this place, and the others like it. Dustin had told me about some kind of barrier. Was he just saying that to keep me from trying to escape? Well, it was time to find out.

The lobby was dark and silent. The receptionist was nowhere to be found. Good. I needed all the luck I could get. Since Dustin had led me outside through the shooting range, I would have to go that way. I hurried through the large gymnasium and into the shooting range.

I reached for the door.

"Lily?"

Dang it. I turned around.

Dustin stood before me, arms crossed and eyebrows raised. "What are you doing here?"

I squared my shoulders, refusing to be intimidated. "I could ask you the same thing."

Looking slightly abashed, he nodded sheepishly at one of the gun slots. "I come here to practice sometimes. Helps me think."

I nodded. "Well, I was just going to check out that basketball court. I've always liked basketball. Care to join me?"

Dustin's eyebrows furrowed in confusion. He and I both knew that I didn't have an athletic bone in my body, but he complied. "OK. Let's go."

"Lead the way," I insisted.

With another suspicious glance at me, he stepped in front of me. His back was turned! I had about ten seconds to make a run for it. But he would probably catch me before I could get too far. Thinking fast, I searched for some kind of object. A flashlight! Dustin had put down his flashlight when we were talking. As quietly and quickly as I could, I grabbed it. Before I could have another second to think, I swung.

Dustin became aware that something was wrong a little too late. Just as he turned around, the flashlight connected with his head. He crumpled to the ground. In sheer panic, I dropped to my knees to check if he was dead. Nope. Just knocked out. He was going to have a serious headache when he woke up. I could already see the lump forming where I had hit him.

"Sorry," I whispered, knowing that he probably couldn't hear me.

After dragging him into a corner, I made a beeline for the door. The cool air felt like a refreshing smack in the face. It woke me up. The adrenaline was pumping now. I still clutched the flashlight, my only weapon.

Taking a deep breath, I headed for the entrance of the school. I had seen people go that direction during the tour. A few people still walked about the grounds, but they were all students. I wasn't surprised that others had decided to break the curfew. However, I couldn't understand why they didn't just leave.

I hurried along, making sure to remain invisible. As I got closer to the entrance, I noticed that I hadn't seen another person for quite some time. That was not a good sign, but I pushed ahead anyway.

"Hey, wait!" someone called.

Without looking back to see who it was, I broke into a sprint. I hadn't gone more than thirty yards when I was suddenly airborne. Then I hit the ground with a sickening thud. The wind knocked out of me, I gasped for air. My head was spinning. When I tried to sit up, my chest burst into a flaming pain that I had never experienced in my life. I clutched at the pain in my chest, continuing to cough and splutter.

I thought I heard some kind of alarm off in the distance somewhere, but there was no way to be sure. My vision was getting blurry. I could no longer form any coherent thoughts. Suddenly all I wanted to do was go to sleep. My eyes drooped until I could see no more.

The first thing I heard was voices. All around me. They sounded so far away and muted, like I was under water. I got the strange feeling that someone was right there beside me. I tried to turn my head, but it was too heavy for me to move. I couldn't even open my eyes. Trying to calm myself, I focused on the voices until they became clear.

"Doctor, you're needed in the emergency room. There was another . . . incident."

"Get a sedative."

"Lily? Are you finally awake?"

Using all my strength, I turned my head to the voice calling my name. I lifted one heavy eyelid, and then the other. As my eyes cleared, a face came into view. I blinked.

"How are you feeling?" Dustin asked, sounding more amused than worried.

I glared at him. "I feel like crap." Eyeing the big bandage on the side of his head, I fought a grin. "How are *you* feeling?"

His hand flew up to his head, eyes turning into slits. "Like I just got hit over the head with a flashlight. Thanks."

My smile faded. "Yeah, I really am sorry for that, but I had to try."

He nodded. "I know."

"So, could you tell me what happened? Everything is kind of a blur."

Dustin's crooked grin grew wider. "Well, after you knocked me out, I suppose you ran for the entrance. Then you hit the barrier. There's a large dome encircling the whole campus. To protect us. Basically, it's a force field. A very strong force field. Everyone knows about it."

I frowned. "Well, how come nobody told me?"

"I did tell you," he patiently reminded me. "Obviously, you didn't listen."

Ignoring his scolding, I tried to prop myself up. I wanted to get a better look at my surroundings.

"I wouldn't do that if I were you," Dustin warned.

He said this a little too late. My chest did not agree with what I was trying to do. Although it wasn't as bad, the pain was still there. Coughing, I fell back in the bed.

"You might have cracked a rib or two," Dustin informed me.

With a groan, I closed my eyes. This could not be happening. "They have a force field around this whole place that's strong enough to crack someone's ribs, and you think it's to keep us safe? You are one messed-up kid." My eyes snapped open to glower at him.

He didn't looked fazed by my insult in the least. In fact, he seemed to be kind of amused. "Lily, of course it's there to protect us. Why else would it be there?"

Not having the energy to argue, I simply shrugged my shoulders, and then winced from the sudden shock of pain. Now that I was more awake, a whole bunch of different aches and pains had started to become very evident.

"I want you to leave now," I said through gritted teeth, trying and failing to hide the agony in my voice.

"Do you need me to call a nurse?" Dustin asked quietly, his amused expression turning into one of pity.

I shook my head. "Please, just go away." I couldn't stand him looking at me like that.

He nodded, starting to get up. "OK, if that's what you want. Don't worry. You'll be out of here in no time."

I simply stared up at the ceiling and continued to do so until he left. As I listened to the sound of his shoes smacking against the floor, I fought the urge to cry. Was I ever going to get out of this place?

THE OTHER GIRL

In addition to my two cracked ribs, my body was riddled with cuts and bruises. It took me several weeks to fully heal, but I was eventually released from the campus hospital. Almost immediately after my release, I was measured, weighed, and put through multiple fitness tests. I also took testing on school stuff like English, social studies, math, science, and decision-making. Some of the decision-making questions were weird, like "If you were stuck in a metal box, what would you do? Explain in full detail."

After the testing, I had a brief meeting with each teacher, where they explained to me what the curriculum would be like for the semester. They all seemed nice enough, some more than others. Like Dustin had said, I was able to choose my curriculum. Since I've always loved a challenge, I chose just about everything that was available: home ec, the normal subjects, Japanese, Latin, dance, martial arts, as well as a few unusual classes, like Hand-to-Hand Combat and Poison 101.

I was enrolled right away. The students I met ranged from six to seventeen. To my surprise, many of them were happy with their current situation. Of course, not everyone was just fine and dandy. Some seemed bitter and angry and kept to themselves. You could see the hatred burning in their eyes every time they would walk past. I didn't blame them, because that was exactly how I felt. Many of them looked at me with pity and hopelessness, like every new kid that came added to their despair. So not everyone had fallen for the trick. They knew something was very wrong.

There was one girl that I especially liked. She was kind of in the middle. She seemed to have come to terms with the fact that there was no escape and had decided to live day by day. She was totally cool. All the kids respected her and came to her for advice. Even the older ones. She would always sit and listen patiently, and all of her answers were wise and calm. It was fascinating just to watch her at work.

One day she approached me. I was sitting on a bench, finishing up an English assignment. Well, at least I was supposed to be. I had begun to draw dresses and outfits of my own creation in the margins. It was free period. She quietly sat down next to me. Up close, she looked surprisingly young. About thirteen or fourteen. Her eyes were a warm chocolate brown. She wore her hair in a loose ponytail.

"Hello," she sang with a friendly smile.

I put up my hand in a greeting.

"You're new here. Correct?"

I nodded slowly, wondering where she was going with this.

"The word around here is you're The Girl," she told me, leaning in.

I stared at her. "What?"

She sighed. "The one that's supposed to take over this whole place with Dustin. You know, and eventually marry him."

I stared at her with my mouth hanging wide open. My heart flew right up into my throat. Gripping the chair, I stammered, "Did you say 'm-marry'?"

She cocked her head. "I'm sorry. I thought you knew. He should have told you that."

"But that can't be. I'm only thirteen! I never even wanted to come here! This cannot be happening. When I find Dustin, he is so dead."

She put her hands on my shoulders. "Whoa. Calm down there." She studied me. "What's your name?"

I told her my name, instantly relaxing. Wow. She really did have special calming powers.

"That's a pretty name, and it's probably partly why you were chosen," she commented.

I looked at her in utter confusion. "What does my name have anything to do with it?"

"Well, you and Dustin's mother share the same name. His dad never did get over her. When he saw your name on your school's roster, it probably caught his attention immediately."

I sat back, the wind knocked right out of me. This just kept getting better and better. "How do you know so much, anyway? Oh, and what's your name?"

The strange girl took a second to collect her thoughts. "First, my name's Cameron. Second, I know so much because

I was supposed to be The Girl. You see, he led me away from my home when I was about nine years old. I was one of the first kids to come to this place. Dustin told me all about himself and his father. I met him about a year after I first arrived."

Whoa. I did not see that one coming. "But if you're supposed to be The Girl, then what the heck am I doing here?"

"Dustin and I weren't really getting along. He's adventurous and reckless, while I'm more of a mellow person. He liked me but not in the way he was supposed to. Once his father saw this, he moved on in a flash. I wasn't mad in the least. Dustin was really very nice to me, but he's not my type."

This took a minute to fully register. So I hadn't been the first girl. Dustin had lied to me again, and of course I had been stupid enough to believe him again. After everything that had happened, you'd think I'd have wised up by now. Apparently not.

Cameron tapped my shoulder. "Lily? Are you there?"

I snapped out of it. "Yeah, unfortunately I am here. Anyway, thanks for telling me all this."

She grinned. "No problem."

A sudden thought came to mind. "Hey, have you ever considered breaking out of this place?"

To my surprise, she didn't stare at me like I was crazy or ask me why in the world she would want to do that. Her face took on a distant look. "Yes, more than once. What I wouldn't give to see my big brother Walter again. He must be in college by now." She came back to earth. "But it's not possible."

To prove her point, she glanced in the direction of the force field surrounding the place. I shuddered, fingering my now-mended ribs. There had to be a way to get out without running into it.

I shook my head, refusing to accept this. "No, there has to be a way out. There always is. I will help you see your brother again."

"You and Dustin are so alike. No wonder he picked you," she answered with a strange smile.

I started to object, but was interrupted by the bell. Cameron stood up and hurried away with a cheerful "Goodbye." I picked up my books in frustration. This whole thing was getting really weird. And lucky me; I was smack in the middle of it all. As I hurried off to class, my mind whirled with the new information. I couldn't wait to give that boy a piece of my mind.

Soon it was the end of the day and there was only one class left. Ironically, the class was beginner's training. Who was my teacher, you may ask? That's right. Dustin. I got dressed in my training suit and headed off to room A109.

He was sitting cross-legged on a mat, with his eyes closed and his hands resting on his knees. I quietly tiptoed toward him. I slowly waved my hand in front of his face. In one rapid movement his hand shot out, taking a hold of my wrist. His eyes flew open, a triumphant smile spreading across his face.

"Nice reflexes," I muttered.

Dustin just studied my face, not letting go of my wrist. We stared at each other for a while, neither of us moving.

"What's wrong?" he asked, letting me go.

I rubbed my wrist, taking a seat next to him. "So, when were you going to tell me about Cameron?" I purposely kept my voice nonchalant and cool.

Dustin sat up stock straight. "Who told you about her?" I couldn't help but enjoy the panic in his voice.

"What does it matter?" I snapped, the coolness gone. "All that matters is that you lied to me. Again."

He shook his head. "I wanted to tell you, but I didn't want to freak you out or anything. I didn't want you to think that I would just dump you like that, because I wouldn't."

Crossing my arms, I said, "That still doesn't explain why you didn't tell me that my name is the same as your mom's and that I'm supposed to marry you. And FYI, we're not even dating! What part of 'stay away from me' did you not get?"

He gawked at me. "You've been talking to Cameron, haven't you?"

I didn't answer, continuing to glare at him with one eyebrow raised.

"Like I said," he finally choked out, "I didn't want to freak you out. Thought it was better if I just didn't tell you. Sorry."

"You should be," I grumbled.

Dustin stood up, holding his hand out for me. "We need to forget about this for right now and start class."

I frowned at his hand. "What if I don't want to?"

"Please?" he coaxed. "In this class, you get to hit me."

That did it. I was suddenly more than happy to participate. Though I didn't let him help me up. I was more than capable of getting up by myself.

We stood facing each other in fighting stances. According to Dustin, it was best that he find out what I already knew before he taught me anything. So we bowed to each other once and then ran at each other.

It was kind of like a dance routine. Punch, punch, kick. Upper cut, upper cut, round house. Spin, back kick, jab. Front kick, backwards spin, cartwheel, smack. (That was my idea.) Back flip, jump kick, bow.

Hands on my hips, I called Dustin a show-off. He smiled slyly and teased that I was just jealous of his awesome skills. As if. With that, we went at it again. This time, I managed to flip Dustin clear over my shoulder. Don't ask how I did it, because to this day I'm still not exactly sure. It just happened.

"Whoa. You're stronger than I thought," he panted.

I shrugged like it was no big deal and helped him up. We had another go.

By the end of training, sweat was rolling down our faces like crazy. The room was silent except for our heavy breathing.

"Nice job," he praised. "I thought I'd have to start with the basics, but you're way more advanced than I expected. Have you ever taken any form of martial arts before?"

"Took some when I was about nine or ten. I liked bowling better, though," I answered.

"Bowling's cool."

I nodded, remembering a certain time I had gone to the local bowling alley with my friends. For some crazy reason, Louis bought six cans of soda and drank every single one down to the last drop. Boy, was he hyper. He was literally bouncing off the walls. Luckily, Mal had her camera phone.

My teacher clapped his hands together. I jumped, coming back to the present.

"Class dismissed," he announced proudly. He enjoyed saying that a little too much. "See you tomorrow. Same time. Same place."

Giving a quick nod, I started for the door. He blocked my way. Looking me straight in the eyes, he apologized for lying and vowed to never do it again.

We were both silent for a minute. He was looking at me in that pleading way again. It was seriously starting to get on my nerves. Suddenly I just wanted to get out of there as fast as I could. I seriously needed to get to my room and start on the big load of homework I had waiting.

"That's a bunch of bull crap," I scoffed.

Before he could answer, I stepped around him, and hurried down the hall without looking back.

BOOT CAMP

The weeks passed by surprisingly quickly. Training became harder and more painful. Now that he knew how good I was, Dustin made it his job to torment me and push me harder than any karate teacher ever would have. He had become more like a teacher than a friend, and a strict one at that. The friendship between Cameron and me grew, but I mostly felt myself turning into a work machine. Every day was the same routine: school, training, homework, and sleep.

There was only one part of the day where I could be myself and relax a little bit, and that was free period, when I talked to Cameron, or sat under a tree and read a book. Sometimes I'd play with the smaller kids and show them some easy combat moves. I think they were beginning to love me almost the same way they loved her.

One particularly tiring day, I had just finished all of my homework and was ready for bed. I quickly changed into my pajamas and rested my head on the pillow. Right when I started to nod off, there was a knock on the door. Groaning, I dragged myself out of bed and answered the door.

"What is it?" I yawned.

"Sorry to bother you," Dustin apologized. "I just wanted to tell you that you've earned this." He handed me a black belt with a golden embroidered lining.

I gingerly traced it with my fingers, fully awake now. A smile tugged at my lips.

He continued to speak. "There's no need for me to train you anymore. You're ready for boot camp. Be dressed and ready to leave by six o' clock. I'll be coming to get you then. Good night." Then he turned to leave.

I grabbed his arm. "Wait a minute. Slow down. Is it really time for me to go already?"

When he saw the worry and confusion on my face, he flashed me a reassuring smile. "Don't worry, everything is going to be fine. I'll tell you more about it in the morning. See you soon."

With that, he bowed and left. I stood in the doorway for a while. The mere thought of going to boot camp made me nervous. There were so many questions I had to ask. I decided to just go back to bed. After all, I had been told that I was to be dressed and ready by six in the morning.

I forced myself to get up at five to pack clothing, toiletries, and books. Then I rushed to brush my teeth, take a shower, and put on fresh clothes before Dustin arrived.

At exactly six o'clock, before he could even knock, I opened the door. He stood there with his hand in a fist poised to knock.

I laughed. "What? Did you think I wouldn't be ready?"

He tried to cover up his surprise. "No, not at all."

Then he offered to carry my bag for me. Defiantly I refused, assuring him that I could carry my own bag, thank you very much. Dustin grinned and backed off. He didn't ask me again.

Unfortunately, the luggage turned out to be extremely heavy, especially since we were walking the whole way there. I had too much pride to admit this, though. While we trudged toward camp, his eyes were on me. I could sense his amusement watching me plow along without a complaint. How very typical.

Just when I thought my knees were about to buckle, there it stood. It looked like a lodge. The words *Boot Camp* glittered in big letters on a sign posted by the front entrance. How original. My former teacher led me to the door. Standing there was the fat-headed bald man that I had seen yelling at those kids when I'd first arrived. He introduced himself as Sergeant Buck. Something told me that this wasn't his real name at all. The sergeant took my bag without even asking and went inside, evidently expecting me to follow.

I turned to Dustin. He shrugged. "Guess this is where we say goodbye for now."

"How long am I supposed to stay here, anyway?" I asked, trying not to panic.

"Oh, just a month or two," he assured me.

I took in a sharp breath. That wasn't exactly what I had wanted to hear. The thought of staying there for a month was downright scary. My face must have given away my fear, because Dustin scrambled to assure me that it wasn't so bad.

According to him, the food was great and the bunks were squeaky clean. All I had to do was stay on the sergeant's good side, do what I was told, and I'd be fine. I wasn't so sure.

With a lump in my throat and a knot in my stomach, I hurried inside before my legs decided to run the other direction. Then I took one last look behind me through the glass double doors. Dustin had already started to trudge back down the hill. With shoulders slumped, hands in his pockets, and head down, he looked kind of . . . I don't know, sad. How could that be, though? He had nothing to be sad about. He finally had me out of his hair for a while. No, he must have been sorry that he didn't have anyone to teach how to fight anymore. I could see how much he loved doing it. His father should have given him that job instead of having him recruit people.

The lobby was wide and spacious. There was a desk and a few chairs. Honestly, I didn't really see a reason for a lobby in a boot camp. Army green was the color theme. Of course. Everything seemed to blend into each other.

Sergeant Buck popped his head in. He told me to stop dawdling and get my sorry fanny moving. I jumped to follow him. Dustin had been right. I really did not want to get on his bad side.

The sergeant led me to a small room that had eight bunk beds. Most of the bunks were already occupied. I picked a lower one by the window.

"Be in the gym at 0800 hours. One of your fellow bunkers will tell you where to go," he shouted in my ear before he left. Really. I don't see why all these sergeants like to shout so much. We're standing right there. Seriously.

Five sets of eyes burned a hole through my back as I unpacked my stuff. When they least expected it, I whirled around to see if they really were staring at me or if I was just being paranoid. They all hurried to go back to what they'd been doing.

Reading seemed to be just about the only thing I could do at the moment, so I sat back on the bunk bed and got started. Turns out that books are good for both reading and spying. The girl across from me had long curly blonde hair. She absentmindedly twirled her hair with her finger and stared into space. The girl in the bunk behind her listened to her iPod. The two top bunkers chatted away. Both had frizzy red hair and freckles. All of them wore a set of a sweatshirt, T-shirt, and shorts with the C.I.A.T. logo.

Soon I got bored of spying and went back to reading. Then something strange and totally unexpected happened. A head from the bunk over me popped out to look at me. It had a smiling face with jet-black pigtails. The skin was a soft milk chocolate.

"How's it goin'?" said the head. "My name's Cattie. What's yours?"

Her hand appeared, reaching out to shake mine. I shook it with caution.

"Hello. I'm Lily Mason."

She giggled with glee as if she was so excited to just find out my name. "Lily. That's a beautiful name. I wish I had a name like that, but no. My name sounds like 'cat.' You know, I never really liked cats. They're so furballish. Is that even a word? Nope. Don't think so. Wow, I made up a word! Have you ever made up a word? Words are so fun. Even the word *word* is cool! You know . . ."

She went on and on, her mouth running like a faucet. It was oddly fascinating to just watch her talk. Cattie had a gift of hopping from one topic to another in about three seconds. I wondered if she liked coffee, because she sure didn't need any.

". . . and that's why I hate vanilla icing," she finally concluded.

I stared at her in disbelief. How the heck had she gotten to that topic? Admittedly, I hadn't really been listening. I was just watching her lips move. You'd think her lips were vibrating, she'd been talking so fast.

Her smile was so full of life that I had to smile back. She made it seem like we weren't at a boot camp at all, just a fun sleepaway camp. Good feelings and buoyancy seemed to emanate from her very being. Her pep was contagious and once in contact, unavoidable.

"Come on up," she insisted. "The top bunk is such a great place for chatting."

So I climbed to the bunk. Cattie was sitting Indian-style. Just like all the other girls, she wore a C.I.A.T. T-shirt and shorts. Beaded bracelets jingled on both arms. Three anklets dangled from her ankles. What kind of boot camp let the students wear that?

"Lay 'em on me," she said, leaning in a little too close.

I leaned back. "What are you talking about?"

She looked at me like I was being stupid. "Questions, of course. I know you have them about this place and all kinds of stuff. Why wouldn't you?"

She had a point there. I could tell she was completely serious, because she didn't say another word. She sat completely still with her eyes set on me, waiting.

"OK, maybe I do have a few questions." I admitted. "First off, how long have you been at boot camp?"

The talkative girl smiled. "I came just last night. Right in time for dinner. The food's really good. Though not as good as my cook, Marie, but—"

I cut her off. "Whoa. Whoa. Whoa. Hold up. You have a cook?"

She nodded. "Uh-huh. You see, before I got here I lived with my mom. She's some kind of politician or something. She used to leave me at home with Marie. We would play games and Marie would make me pastries and cakes. It was simply stupendous!" Cattie paused, reminiscing about the golden days. Then her smile turned into a frown. "But then Mom started to think that leaving me home with Marie wasn't good enough. She hired babysitter after babysitter, but still she wasn't satisfied. Then she met the headmaster of this school. He told her all about his 'plans for the future' and offered to take me in. A few days later I arrived here."

She flashed a megawatt smile, but it seemed kind of forced. Her eyes smoldered with rage. To tell you the truth, it kind of frightened me a bit. Then she blinked and her eyes were back to normal.

I cleared my throat uneasily. "How long have you been here? Like, in this whole place."

Cattie furrowed her eyebrows, thinking. "Umm, I'd say about four months. You know, all these months and I still haven't met the amazing Recruiter, A.K.A. Dustin, the headmaster's son. Have you?"

Before I could so much as open my mouth to speak, she slapped her palm to her forehead. "Well, duh, you're The Girl."

"Does everybody know about me?" I inquired, lowering my voice to a hushed whisper.

"Of course," she whispered back. "Why wouldn't everybody know about you? You're all we've talked about since you got here."

Just great. I sighed. This was not the sort of fame that I wanted. In my daydreams, the whole world knew my name from magazines and TV screens. Yes, everybody knew Lily Mason the fashion designer and part-time musician who'd made a stunning singing debut. But never in my wildest dreams had I been known for this, being some kind of future queen of a horrible organization that I had no intention of ruling.

The chatterbox frowned. "You OK there? You look a little sick. Maybe you should visit the nurse. She's very nice, really. I'll bring you to her. Don't worry. We're allowed."

I started to tell her that I was perfectly fine when her watch beeped. All the girls' watches were beeping. They immediately began to tie their hair up and take off their jewelry.

Cattie glanced at her watch. "Shoot. It's time to get to the gym. Come on, follow me." She appraised me up and down. "You need to change your clothes. Open your bag. They probably gave you a uniform."

I opened my bag and sure enough, there they were. Along with a watch like theirs. It too was beeping. Quick as a wink, I got dressed and secured the watch around my wrist. We marched out in a neat little line. The red-haired twins no longer chatted, but played a poking game. They kept stealing smug glances at each other and then me, giggling secretively like they knew some big inside joke.

The corridors were long and narrow. When we finally entered the gym, I felt like I was about to explode. Those girls were seriously getting on my nerves with all that giggling, and I was sure the others felt the same way. Then I took a look around. A loud gasp escaped my lips before I could stop myself. I ignored the even louder chortles now coming from more than just the two redheads. The room had to be at least as big as two football fields. Hurdles, tires, shoots, ropes, sparring mats, and a whole bunch of other stuff hung from the ceilings and was scattered around the floor. Sergeant Buck stood right in the middle of it all, completely still. He didn't even blink, his face stony and expressionless. I swear, he could have been a statue.

Everyone filed in. Some kids I had seen around the premises. Others I had never seen before in my life. They all wore the same set of clothing, like a uniform. Since all the other kids stood as still as the sergeant, I tried to do the same.

He slowly walked along the line of boys and girls, glaring at each and every one of us. "Today you train inside. Tomorrow will be a different story. I don't care if it's raining, snowing, hailing, or if there's a tornado. All of you, and I mean *all* of you, will be outside workin' your butts off tomorrow. Do you understand?!"

We all yelled, "Yes, sir!" at the top of our lungs. Then we split up into the lines we had arrived in and stood at attention to wait for his orders.

Sergeant Buck started shouting out stations for us to go to. I hurried along after my fellow bunkers. We had been sent to the giant net that went all the way up to the ceiling. At the very top, there was a buzzer that you were supposed to hit. A large mat had been placed at the bottom, but that wouldn't help if someone fell from all the way up there. I looked around to see if there was any kind of harness or anything like that. Of course, there was not.

My bunkmates stared at the huge net. One of the redheads cursed under her breath. The blonde girl looked like she was about to faint. I shot a glance toward Cattie. She stood there with her mouth open and her head tilted upward, just staring up at the thing.

Sighing, I said, "Well, if no one else is going up, I guess I'll go first."

The girls stared at me as I sauntered right on up to the net. Once my hands and feet were secure, I began to climb. When

I was about halfway up, I started to feel kinda confident. That is, until Cattie so very kindly reminded me not to look down. I looked down. Everyone appeared to be tiny from up there. It was cool, but then I got dizzy. My vision grew slightly blurry and the room spun. My grip loosened, stomach flopping. I shivered and completely lost my hold for a moment. Drawing in a surprised breath, I frantically grasped at the net.

"She's gonna fall!" I heard someone say.

Determined to prove them wrong, I managed to get a good hold on the net again. Before plowing on, I took a deep breath, tuning out everything around me. Nothing was going to stop me from touching that buzzer. After a great deal of heaving and climbing, I finally had the pleasure of slamming my hand on it. The girls cheered as I climbed back down, which was even scarier.

By the time I had gotten down, the sergeant stood among them. He took a step toward me. I stiffened and stood at attention. Unfortunately, he kept coming toward me until he was uncomfortably close. He towered over me, glaring.

"I suppose you think you're all that now," he spat, his expression hard.

I began to say, "No, sir," but he cut me off. "You're not. You are just a scruffy little kid like the rest. So don't expect any favors, kid."

He walked away, probably to drown some other person's spirits.

The iPod girl patted me on the shoulder. "Hey, don't sweat it. That's his way of complimenting you. You did great up there. My name's Trudence, by the way. True for short."

She had a splash of brown freckles on her face and a mane of sandy hair. She waved and smiled at me as she went up next.

After everyone had their turn on the Net O' Horror, we moved on to the next station: the dreaded ropes. That was the one thing I could never do in P.E. True saw me staring at it like death itself and asked me what was wrong. I told her my dilemma.

"Just try your best. If you don't even try, you'll get into serious trouble," she said.

I nodded, watching one of the terribly tiresome twins climb up the rope like some kind of monkey. Boy, was she fast. The other twin stood right under her, squealing and clapping with delight. Cattie and True rolled their eyes at the same time.

Soon it was my turn. I gulped and put my hands around the rope. Pulling myself up took just about all of my strength. I tried and tried until my hands were raw. Just when I was near the top, I slid right back down. My hands really stung now, the palms bright red from rope burn.

Cattie took a look at my hands over my shoulder. "Ooh. That looks like it hurts. You really should go to the nurse for that. I had to go last night for an injury. She has everything. Bandages, antibiotics, shots—you name it, she has it. Once, when I was in third grade, my friend and I were playing hopscotch and . . ."

We all stopped listening and started to move on to the next station. She followed, still chattering to no one in particular. I stared at my hands. They seemed to sting even more. True urged me to ask to go to the nurse, so I hesitantly called the sergeant over. I showed him my hands. He told me to suck it up until training was over.

I joined the group, fuming.

"Wow, he's being really hard on you," Cattie mused.

No, really? Thank you, Captain Obvious.

True snapped her fingers, making me jump. "I know why."

She had our full attention.

"Well, it's most likely because you're The Girl. He's testing you to see if you're up to it. Can't believe I didn't think about that before."

Weary of all this "The Girl" talk, I groaned. This whole thing was seriously getting on my nerves. Everywhere I went, that stupid name seemed to follow. Who even came up with that? What, did they get it from some kind of movie or something? Seriously. They could have at least come up with a better name.

The rest of training was a whirlwind of sit-ups, crunches, push-ups, and other grueling torture. By the time Sergeant Buck blew the very loud whistle, my whole body ached. I was in so much pain that I could barely feel the rope burn anymore.

Even when I protested that all I needed was rest, both True and Cattie insisted that I go to the nurse. So they led me down some hallways and through some rooms. The word NURSE had been written in big letters on the door. She was a tiny but strongly built woman. She seemed friendly enough.

"Hello. Call me Karen. Let's see what we have here."

She took a look at my now blazing red palms. Nurse Karen clucked her tongue and reached for some ointment. It was cool and slimy against my skin, but the stuff made my hand feel better.

While she slathered it on, I took a peek around the room. Rows and rows of medicines, ointments, bandages, and just about everything else lined the starch-white walls. There was a comfortable cot in the back of the room. All was neat and had been carefully organized.

"There you go," said the nurse once she'd finished. "In a few hours, that nasty rope burn will be gone for good."

I thanked her and, with one more appraising look around, left the room. Outside, I met up with True and Cattie. We headed back to our room.

"So," Cattie started, nudging me. "Tell us about Dustin." The last thing I wanted to do was talk about him, but they both stared at me expectantly. With an exasperated sigh, I agreed to tell them about him when we got back.

So, once in our room, we all piled onto Cattie's bunk bed. I started from the beginning; when I first met him. The whole room turned silent as I told my story. Somehow I knew everyone was listening, not just True and Cattie. They hung on every word, squealing with fright or sighing at certain times. I felt like I was at a sleepover, gushing about some boy from school. Throughout the storytelling, I was interrupted quite a lot. Mostly by Cattie with remarks such as *Wow, he*

*sounds so dreamy.... What?! I so can't believe he did that.... I can't
believe you did that!... How come you went there?*

And so on. I soon learned to ignore the comments.

When I finished, all eyes were trained on me. I squirmed
under their awed gazes. My chatty friend broke the silence by
drowning me with a flood of questions. The rest of the girls
groaned and left us to talk amongst ourselves.

"I think he sounds like a conceited jerk. Look at what he's
done to you. There's no way you can possibly believe he cares
about you at all," said True.

Cattie bit her lip. "I don't know about that. Maybe he's
not all that bad. I mean, he does sound really dreamy and
maybe he's nice."

True began to say something but I put my hand up to stop
her. Then I turn my gaze toward Cattie. "It doesn't matter
how dreamy he is. He still brought me here, knowing what
would happen. Then he lied to me again. You know what? I
don't even know what he wants from me. Dustin told me what
his father wanted, but he didn't say anything about what *he*
wanted. The truth is, I don't even care anymore. I just wanna
get out of here and take as many people as I can with me."

"That's a tall order," True remarked. There was mischief
in her eyes. "You might need some help with that, and I don't
mean to brag, but I'm pretty good at cookin' up schemes."

I smiled, catching on quick. "You really want to help me?"

She shrugged. "Sure."

We both looked at Cattie. For once, she seemed
completely silent. She refused to raise her eyes from the floor.

Then she began to speak, stating that it was different for her, since her mom had sent her here. Maybe this place wasn't so bad and maybe we were wrong. She had even heard rumors that we would eventually be set free.

Putting my hands on her shoulders and staring straight into her eyes, I told her about the day Dustin and I had come across that scary building. In detail, I described the stretcher and the little girl that lay unconscious on it.

With a grim expression, she appeared to make a decision. "I'm in."

So now all we needed was a plan. True came up with the idea that I should gain Dustin's trust and then, when he least expected it, knock him over the head or something. I asked her what the heck that was supposed to do. Then Cattie calmly stated that I would need a gun. Uh-uh. That was out of the question.

But before I could protest, she talked over me. "Don't worry. I've seen all the James Bond movies and stuff like that. It's usually that the woman's captured; she, like, knocks him over the head or something. Then she takes his gun and pulls it out on him, forcing him to release her."

I loathe guns. This is why James Bond and all action movies aren't exactly on my top ten list. I insisted that there had to be another way. Something that didn't involve guns.

Both True and Cattie scrunched up their faces in concentration. In about five minutes they came up with a verdict. There was no other way unless I could persuade Dustin to help me. We all knew that was highly unlikely. So grudgingly I gave in. Now we just needed to figure out how to gain access to the weaponry.

Soon the girls and I had come up with a ludicrous outline of what was to happen. The watches went off once again. Just like before, everyone got up and headed out the door in single file. Someone informed me that it was time for lunch. Despite the things I had been told, images of slop and mystery meat came to mind. My stomach grumbled in hunger and disgust.

When we entered the lunchroom, I was pleasantly proven wrong. The tables, chairs, and floors had not a speck of grime. Children and teens alike were sitting down, chatting excitedly about their day. Despite the cold, dreary atmosphere of the camp, this room felt warm. Inviting, even. Although some tough-looking men and women surrounded the perimeter, all stood at ease.

Our bunk stood in line for food. I observed that we were not served, but rather chose for ourselves. There was a long salad bar filled with different greens, veggies, dressings, toppings, and fruits. Standing next to it was a sandwich bar with a surplus of cold cuts and every kind of bread known to man. Next to that, I could see an assortment of soups, chilies, and other hot foods. Finally, at the end of all that were the drinks. The choices were water, iced tea, Gatorade, lemonade, and fruit punch. For some reason, seeing all that food made it very hard for me not to smile. The same thing seemed to be happening to everyone else too.

I chose a seat by the window, my plate full, but not too full. I didn't want to look like a pig or anything. Cattie and

True soon joined me. Since we were all really hungry, we ate in silence for a while. I figured that the suited people bordering the walls were there for intimidation. It was working. Every few minutes a person would stop eating for a second and steal a quick uneasy glance in their direction. I too eyed the stock-still strangers.

When I was done eating, my eyes drifted to the window. Not a cloud in the sky. The grass was no longer frozen. It looked rather tempting. I found myself longing to go outside.

True followed my gaze. "Oh, we'll be going outside soon enough." She didn't sound too happy about that.

"Yeah," Cattie chimed in, "to do some drills or something."

I made a face. That didn't sound very fun. What did I expect? This was boot camp after all. For the rest of lunch, we chatted about silly stuff, like the first thing we would do when we got out of this place. We talked about sleepovers and birthday parties. I told them about my family and friends back at home. They giggled at the funny things I said about Louis, and were solemn when I remembered the time Malerie's dog died. As I laughed and ate with them, I realized that these girls reminded me so much of my friends. They had my back and made me the happiest I'd been since I'd arrived at this dreary place. It was hard to believe that I had just met them that morning.

Lunch ended and soon after came the drills. Our afternoon was spent doing push-ups, crunches, knee-highs, sit-ups, weights, and running laps. I had never worked so hard in my life. Gym had never been nearly as grueling as this.

After about fifty crunches, my stomach was tight and sore. My arms hurt terribly from the weights, and I could no longer feel my legs. Sweat dripped down my face by the gallon. The ground looked so comfortable, I wished that I could just lie right there and rest. I didn't dare, though. Sergeant Buck would have had a fit.

The sky had turned from baby blue to indigo when we were finally allowed to stop. Water bottles were handed out. I drank all the water in one big gulp, wiping the sweat from my brow. Legs unsteady, I wobbled to the line forming at the door. All the others were just about as run-down as I was. Some were leaning over and puking, and others had passed out. I was close to doing both of those things myself.

Once we were back in our room, I stiffly got into my bunk, falling asleep instantly. A few minutes later, I was being shaken awake. I groggily swatted my hand at the gentle hand on my shoulder.

"Lily," a voice whispered, "they're totally gonna freak if you don't come to dinner."

My eyes slowly opened to find Cattie standing over me. Wincing, I rose from the bed and followed her out.

I stifled a yawn as I stood in line for food. I was so tired that I didn't pay any attention to what I was putting on my plate. When I sat down, even the hard table seemed like a pillow. So I laid my head on the table for just a second. The next thing I knew, a loud whistle was being blown in my ear. That woke me up a bit and scared the living daylights out of me. My hand automatically brought the fork to my lips, shoveling it all in.

My friends practically had to drag me out of there when dinner was over. I couldn't keep my eyes open anymore. I was asleep before I even hit the covers.

A loud horn sounded, blowing me right out of bed. Since every bone in my body still ached, this didn't feel too great. I crawled back to bed, rubbing the sleep from my eyes. There was a deluge of shrieking girls, running to the bathrooms. Water ran in the showers as people poured in. When I finally got to the mirror and saw my reflection, I nearly jumped out of my skin. I looked like the living dead. As usual, my hair was in disarray. There were bags under my eyes and I could see visible bruises from the previous day of drills. I washed my face and brushed my teeth until they gleamed.

Surprisingly, the shower water felt warm against my skin. It soothed my bruises and sore muscles. I scrubbed diligently in order to scrape away all the grit and grime from the previous day.

After having a good wash and putting on fresh clothes, I went for breakfast. Then I carried my tray of a buttered roll, scrambled eggs, bacon, and orange juice to the usual spot.

"Good morning," Cattie sang with a smile. "You seem to be in high spirits."

"I like the showers," I answered.

True nodded in agreement. "Great, aren't they? Not to sound weird or anything, but I like to go there to think."

"Really? Okay. I can see how that would work," I said.

Cattie stared at us like we were a couple of whack jobs. "You do know that you're talking about showers, right?"

True and I broke into a fit of giggles. Our ravings about the showers sounded like we were talking about some kind of spa. While hugging my stomach and giggling uncontrollably, I caught a glimpse out the window. My giggles immediately stopped. True and Cattie turned their heads to see what I was staring at.

The sun shone so brightly you'd think it was a summer day. Was it? When I'd first arrived, it had been so cold that I had nearly frozen to death.

My smile faded. "What month is it?"

True's face, still frozen in laughter, turned to a frown. "I dunno. February or March maybe?"

I'd arrived in December. Had it really been that long? The mood at our table changed drastically. I didn't feel like laughing anymore. I felt like doing the opposite. The effects of the soothing warm water were wearing off and my aches and pains were becoming evident again. What was also becoming evident was the need to get back to our plan to get out. So what if the food was great and I liked the showers? The time to act was now. My realization of how long I'd been here only fueled my determination. I looked up at the girls, my fingers gripping the side of the table. The same affirmation showed on their faces as well. Relaxing, I sighed and took a bite of the roll. We were all on the same page.

A loud voice made me jump. One of the sergeants was yelling for us to get off our butts and head out. Heart thumping, I hurried out the door with everyone else.

Bulky guys stood at the doorway, giving orders. We stood against the wall at attention as ordered. Then Sergeant Buck arrived. He hadn't come alone. A severe-faced woman stood on one side of him, while an even meaner-looking man stood on the other. They appeared younger than the sergeant, in either their late twenties or early thirties.

Standing directly behind them was the biggest, cruelest obstacle course that I had ever seen. There was a huge rock wall that had real jagged rocks instead of fake ones. The monkey bars weren't even kid safe! With a height of about thirty feet, each bar had been made of rusted metal. Instead of going ten bars across, it went about forty. If you were unfortunate enough to fall off, you would drop straight into a mud pit. Near the monkey bars were two rows of big flat tires stretched so far apart, it had to be almost impossible to hop through unless you used your whole body. To get to the zip line, you'd have to climb over another rock wall even taller than the last one. Once off the zip line, there was a giant shoot that led to the barbed wire, which was so low to the ground I had no idea how we were supposed to crawl under that without getting cut into shreds. Maybe that was the point. The hurdles came after the barbed wire. There was simply no way anyone could get over them unless they had the skills to jump really high or had very long legs.

When the obstacle course ended, it opened into fields and fields of grass. Placed twenty yards apart from each other stood wooden signs. On these signs were different kinds of instructions. For example, one said to do thirty push-ups.

Before I could finish reading the signs, the sergeant began to speak. "Attention! Listen up, 'cause I'm not repeating myself."

He cleared his throat. Then he introduced the two people on either side of him. The woman's name was Lieutenant Kantanker; the man was Lieutenant Parker. They both swept their cold unfeeling eyes over us. They'd be stationed at certain spots to "cheer" us on.

We were all reluctant to start, so we had to get yelled at. The rocks scraped at my hands and knees. I held my breath the whole time I was on the monkey bars. I made sure that I had a good grip on each rung before moving on. Lieutenant Kantanker screamed in my ear the whole time. It was more of an annoyance than encouragement.

My downfall came at the push-ups. My muscles were still really sore from before, and I've never been a stellar athlete. So after fifteen push-ups, I just dropped. My arms couldn't take the weight anymore. Because I had stopped, I was forced to start the course all over again. To have come so far and have to start again was devastating. With a sigh of despair, I jogged back toward the beginning.

For two more hours this went on. Even if we went through the course with no mistakes, we still had to do it over and over. Because of this constant painful cycle, my arms were extremely tired. This turned out to be a problem when it came to the dreaded monkey bars of doom. I ended up covered with mud from head to toe.

Once we went back inside, everything in my body ached yet again. Moans and groans could be heard throughout the group. They were quiet ones, of course, since no one wanted to get on the sergeant's bad side.

I took as long of a shower as I could take. Although I got all the mud off, I still didn't feel too great. None of us did. True grunted in pain.

"Stupid obstacle course," she grumbled. "And to think, we still have to do those horrible drills soon."

I groaned. "Ugh, don't remind me."

While we complained about our many ailments, Cattie remained absolutely silent. Of course, we noticed this and asked her what was wrong.

"I forgot to tell you something," she confessed. "Something important."

"Well, come on. Spit it out!" I urged.

"I was sneaking around the grounds last night," she let out in a rush.

True and I stared at her openmouthed. Was she out of her mind? Did she realize what would have happened if she had gotten caught?

She looked down at our hands. "I know. I know. It's just that I needed a place to think, too, and I like taking walks, so I thought, why not? Then I got to thinking that maybe while

I was there I could look for weapons. Every boot camp has a stash somewhere." She paused to build up the suspense. "I started tiptoeing and dodging behind walls like a real-life secret agent. Just when I was about to give up, wham! There they were. Rows and rows of 'em."

She sat back, finished with her story, obviously proud of what she had discovered.

This was indeed good news, but also bad. Would our crazy scheme really work? Lowering my voice, I told them my plan of what to do next. About a day or two before we left camp, we'd have to sneak out at night. Then we would each take one weapon for ourselves. Someone would have to be the lookout. That would be Cattie. For fun, we named our plan Mission Impossible IV: Project A. We'd take the weapons with us when we left boot camp, but we'd have to use them quickly before we were caught with them.

Having time to kill before lunch, the girls and I played a game of Would You Rather.

The tiring days went by quickly. Nearly every day was the same. I soon became accustomed to the routine. As the weeks progressed, I found myself aching less and less even though the training was as brutal as ever. I guessed that I was getting used to the pain, since now I just felt numb. My arms and legs became stronger and the little scabs and scars accumulated on my body. Besides the grueling drills, horrible obstacle course, and the terrible feeling of confinement, it really wasn't all that bad.

STEALTH

On the night before the departure ceremony, I was very jumpy. What if we got caught? Would we get some kind of horrific punishment, or worse, be forced to stay longer? Sheer panic crashed over me in waves as I lay awake. I glanced around the room. Everyone seemed to be asleep. The blonde girl—never did catch her name—snored softly in the bunk across from mine. Red tufts of hair stuck out from the covers on the two top bunks. The silence made me even more antsy.

Finally, I couldn't take it anymore.

"Cattie, are you awake?" I whispered, lightly kicking the bunk above me. "Don't you think we should be leaving now?"

I heard what sounded like a muffled "Ouch!" Then there was a rustling of sheets. Her head appeared from the top bunk, hair disheveled.

"Yes, I'm awake," she hissed. "And a little sore on the bottom, thanks to you. I have a cousin who—"

"All right. I'm sorry. I'm just nervous," I apologized.

She nodded. "I'm nervous too. Come on, let's get out of here." She climbed down the ladder. I noticed that she was already dressed, like me. We woke True up and headed out as quietly and quickly as possible.

The hallways were eerily silent. True and I followed Cattie down the corridors, looking this way and that. When we came near the third door on the left, we heard voices. From what I could gather, some of the staff was having a midnight snack of some kind. Out of pure curiosity, we pressed our ears to the door.

"Just think, by tomorrow those brats will be gone," one said with a satisfied sigh.

"Yeah," barked another one. "But a new batch will be arriving soon after."

There were agitated murmurs of agreement.

Someone cleared her throat angrily. "These 'brats' are mere children who are being forced to do things no one their ages should be doing. However, they continue to work hard and push themselves to the limit. Many of them come to me with ghastly injuries, but they don't utter a single cry of pain. They just stare down at the floor, trying very hard not to show any emotion."

We couldn't believe our ears. Someone was actually taking our side. An uncomfortable silence followed.

Finally Sergeant Buck muttered, "Tough little monsters. I'll give them that."

Again there was silence and a few uneasy coughs. After a while they began to talk about other things, such as politics and how much they were getting paid, which was a lot, mind you.

I felt like kicking myself for spending so much time standing there. Still, it definitely was interesting to hear what they really thought about us. Brats? Tough little monsters, were we? Oh, I'd show them how tough we really were. I'd outwit them and teach them a thing or two. I squared my shoulders, holding my head a little higher. We silently moved on.

It felt like a full hour before Cattie stopped us in front of a big metal door. When she tried to turn the knob, it wouldn't open.

"I don't understand. It opened for me before and I'm sure this is the right one," she insisted, staring at the door in disbelief.

With my hands on my hips, I asked, "Are you sure nobody saw you?"

She blinked. "Of course."

True rolled her eyes, removing a bobby pin from her hair. In one stride, she stood right in front of the door. She picked the lock and had the door open in a matter of seconds.

We entered the room, which was full of weaponry. One word: Awful. Guns, grenades, and heaven knows what else lined the walls. I didn't really understand why they would have all this stuff. I mean, this was a boot camp, but technically not a real one. And another question: Why wasn't their security better? We had just picked the lock and waltzed right in. There should have been sirens going off and red lights flashing. Something. Anything. The lack of protection was shocking and a bit suspicious. Maybe they had a hidden camera somewhere and a mob of angry armed men would be coming this way any minute, but when I looked out the door, there was nothing. Since we'd left our room, we'd seen no one patrolling the hallways. The whole setup seemed very unprofessional.

As planned, Cattie stood at the door while True and I raided the stash. I settled on a handgun. Although it made me grimace to touch it, I reluctantly slipped it into the bag I'd brought with me. True took one for herself and one for Cattie as well. Then she took a few other things that she thought would be useful.

Before leaving the room, I took a quick sweep around just to make sure that there weren't any big gaps or anything that indicated that someone had been there. Nope. We'd been careful to take very little so that we wouldn't leave any clues behind. Being surrounded by all those terrible tools made me feel oddly vulnerable. I hightailed it out of there once Cattie gave the go-ahead. My friends and I surreptitiously crept down the corridors extra quietly until we were safely back in our room.

The other two fell asleep instantly, but I did not. Lying awake, I checked my watch. 1:00 a.m. exactly. I willed myself to go to sleep. Since the departure ceremony was tomorrow, the time to wake up had been changed to an earlier time. Like the staff had said, they couldn't wait to get rid of us "brats." Huh. Clenching my teeth, I replayed the whole conversation in my head. They made me sick. We weren't so crazy about them either. On that note, I slipped into a deep sleep.

I wandered the halls of KVMS, my school. Hearing sounds coming from the now dark cafetorium, I headed there. Chase, Malerie, Louis, Asialie, and Ella sat at one of the lunch tables. They had their heads lowered, voices hushed. I stepped closer to hear what they were saying. They abruptly stopped whispering, turning to stare at me. Elated to see them again, I felt like running over and giving them all a great big hug, but something stopped me in my tracks. Their expressions were all wrong. Instead of smiles, looks of fear and perplexity greeted me.

"Lily," I heard a voice say, "don't do anything hasty. Just put it down and we'll work this out."

I turned to see Dustin slowly backing away from me, hands up. "Please, don't shoot!" He got down on his knees, eyes pleading. "I'll do anything. Look, I'm sorry for everything I've done. You're right to be mad, just please don't shoot."

Bewildered by this peculiar spectacle, I tried to assure him that I had no idea what he was talking about. I had no intention of hurting him. Dustin didn't believe me. He continued to beg and whimper. This was so unlike him. Then I saw it. That thing in my hand. My shaking hand was pointing it right at him.

"No," I whispered, trying to put my arm down, but it wouldn't budge. Panicking, I attempted to drop the thing, but it was as if it was glued to my palm. Shaking with fear, I tried to throw it, stomp on it, and bang it against the wall. Nothing worked.

I had no choice but to watch in horror as my fingers slowly pulled the trigger. Crying silently, I closed my eyes, unable to bear what came next. There was a loud bang and I felt my hand being pushed back from the force. After an agonizing cry, I heard nothing. Finally free of the dirty thing, my sweaty hand let it fall to the ground.

Opening my eyes, I ran toward the lifeless heap on the ground. The utter silence threatened to suffocate me as I placed his head upon my lap. A scream for him to get up filled my lungs, but nothing came out. I held him close, tears streaming down my cheeks. How could this be happening? This had never been the plan! He wasn't supposed to be . . . I couldn't even think the word.

Suddenly my friends had surrounded me. Their looming figures glared at me in disapproval. They chanted something that I couldn't quite hear. Their voices became louder and louder until my ears rang with the terrible screeching.

"Murderer!" my former friends accused, pointing their fingers at me.

I noticed that my hands were wet. Turning my palms over, I found them scarlet red with blood. This time my screams bounced against the walls, making an echo. Agony, surprise, fear, and a whole bunch of other emotions surged through me all at the same time. Darkness closed in as the now ghoulish figures came closer and closer. Soon I could see nothing but their feet and grasping hands. So many hands. Certain that my life would soon end, I squeezed my eyes shut and waited.

I woke up in a cold sweat, the sheets in disarray. I could still feel the blood on my palms and the shame that pulsed inside me. Wincing at the sound of the stupid morning horn, I rubbed at my eyes and stretched. In the shower, I scrubbed a little harder to wash that horrible dream away. Remembering the look in his eyes and all that blood made me shiver. I gave myself a vigorous shake. Scrubbing wasn't doing any good, so

I tried just blocking it out of my head. That seemed to work for the time being. Satisfied, I finished getting ready and headed for the ceremonial breakfast feast.

Laughter and excited chatter streamed out of the room. Everything about it was bigger and friendlier. Yes, the dining room had always been the happiest place, but this was different. We were finally going to leave! This made everyone happy—especially the staff, as we had learned the previous night.

I sat down at the usual place, greeting my friends as cheerfully as I could. They weren't buying it. I assured them that nothing was wrong. Then after much persistence on their part, I caved. I told them about my dream.

"I know what it means," Cattie said with a casual nod of the head.

True and I both stared at her.

She took a sip of her fruit punch before going on. "It's your conscience." She leaned back in her chair, looking all wise and knowing.

"That explains it," I agreed. "I really don't want to do this, so I think my brain is reminding me of that. Maybe there is another way . . ."

True shook her head. "Sorry, Lily, but there's not. It's not like you're going to hurt the guy. You'll just hold him at gunpoint to make him get us out of here like in the movies. Anyway, we can't come up with a whole new plan now. We leave boot camp in a few hours!"

"But this isn't a movie! It's real life. I mean, how is our crazy scheme going to hold up?"

"It will," Cattie insisted, putting her hand over mine. "If we trust in each other, then we can do anything."

True raised her eyebrows. "Did you get that from a sappy movie or something?"

Cattie grinned. "Yeah."

We all giggled. It was a little corny, but she was right. We really could do anything if we had the drive to do it. I had full confidence in them and myself. This had to work.

"Fine, we'll stick to the original plan. If anything changes, I'll find a way to contact you, all right?" I said.

They both nodded their heads. We stacked our hands on the table and broke on three. Nothing could stop us now. The confidence emanating from them lifted my spirits. Not entirely, though. I couldn't quite shake the guilt tugging at me. Grandmother had always said that if something didn't sit right, then it was wrong. Biting my lip, I gazed out the window. Maybe that dream had been telling me something.

A loud bugle interrupted my thoughts. The ceremonies had begun. Everyone lined up in a single file. Down the halls we marched until we reached the ballroom. Why a boot camp would have a ballroom stumped me, but there it was. Streamers and balloons covered the huge ceiling. The floors were as shiny as Asialie's lip gloss. A sharp pang of homesickness surprised me. I shook it off and stood at attention like the rest.

Sergeant Buck walked down the line of unusually stiff children, handing out metals. They weren't the cheap kind. No, they sparkled and shined with real gold and silver.

"Never have I seen a sorrier group of ragamuffins," he

growled. "However, you are tough, and tough is what this place is about. We've decided to give you kids a little treat." With the way he said "kids," you'd think he was talking about a bunch of cockroaches.

He glared down at us. "Since you've been working so hard, and it's the last day, you may mingle with your friends and have some punch and refreshments."

With that, we were let loose into the big room. Music blared, but nobody danced. They just hung around the punch table, munching on cookies. People mumbled to their friends, staring down at the ground.

"That's it," True exclaimed, taking another swig of her punch and slamming it down. "I've had enough of this. Time to liven up this dead party."

Cattie and I followed her to the center of the room, wondering what the heck she was doing. All eyes were on us.

Then True began to dance. I'm not kidding. She was dancing like a crazy person in the middle of a dead party. She looked over at me like she wanted me to do something. So I got in there and started to dance right beside her. Then she stopped and said, "Go, Lily!" She stepped back next to Cattie, who had begun to chant along with her.

Soon everyone had surrounded me in a circle, chanting, "Go, Lily!" Then some guy I'd never seen before jumped in, dancing with me. Shrugging my shoulders, I went with it. Whatever. Following our lead, they all joined in.

"You're a good dancer," said the guy.

"Thanks. Right back at you," I yelled over the music. And I meant it.

For the first time, I looked him over. He rocked a buzz cut and a strong build. He appeared to have a love for dancing, like me. I decided that I'd like to get to know this boy.

After a while I got tired and excused myself to the refreshment table. On my way over, I caught a glimpse of my pal True. She was teaching a group of boys how to beat box. She seemed to be having fun. When I reached the table, I found Cattie talking some poor soul to death. I sipped my punch and took a bite of a brownie, watching in amusement.

"Anyway, then I went to the carnival and got a cool keychain. Wanna see?" she was saying.

When she turned to get it out of her pocket, the girl fled the scene. Cattie noticed that she was gone, shrugged, and moved on to another person. I laughed, shaking my head.

I spotted my dancing partner and walked over to him. I leaned on the wall next to him. "Hey."

"Hey, what's up?" he said in a friendly manner.

"Nothin' much." I replied, nonchalantly sipping my punch. " I was just wondering what your name was."

"Marcus," he said. Then he sized me up. "Aren't you Dustin's girlfriend?"

"No, I'm not Dustin's girlfriend. I will never be his girlfriend and don't you forget it," I snapped.

Marcus raised his arms. "Whoa. No need to get mad. I was just askin' since I've seen you around and Dustin told me about you."

"Really? Are you guys, like, friends or something?"

He shoved his hands in his pockets. "Guess you can say

that. He took me off the streets and brought me here. We've been kinda like brothers ever since."

"So, you like it here?"

He shrugged. "At least I don't have to worry about food and stuff like that. It's cool."

I had nothing to say to that. We were silent for a while until Marcus asked me if I liked it there.

"Not really. I just wanna go home."

"Too bad you feel that way. I actually never met anyone who didn't wanna be here."

"If you don't mind me asking, how did you learn to dance like that?" I inquired.

He explained that his brother had taught him. That's how they made money. People would pay to see them dance and do acrobatics. Then he asked me the same question.

"Taught myself. So, where's your brother now?"

Oh no. I had asked the wrong question. He looked down at his shoes, digging his hands even deeper into his pockets. "He's dead."

"Oh. I'm so sorry," I said, wishing that I hadn't been so nosy.

"Naw, it's cool," he assured me with a halfhearted shrug. "Happened a long time ago."

Before I could say anything else, the horn sounded, saving us from an inevitable awkwardness. After saying goodbye to Marcus, I gladly followed the crowd out the door.

Cool air hit my face as I entered the outside world, and it looked like it was about to rain. I sniffed the lovely air, holding out my arms with a happy smile. No more drills and horrible obstacle courses. No longer would my body ache every night and every minute of the day. And best of all, no more grown-ups screaming in my ear or telling me to drop and give them fifty. The thought made me so giddy that I could've shouted.

Before I could do just that, True appeared beside me.

"Remember the plan," was all she said before running off somewhere.

I nodded to myself, all giddiness gone. I would never forget the plan. That was the only chance of my escape. When I remembered what I was supposed to do to make it all work, I felt nauseous. I wanted nothing more than to take that thing out of my bag and fling it somewhere. I didn't, of course, though I wished I could.

I began to walk in the direction of the school, deciding to take my time. The other kids whizzed past me while I kept a slow pace. Soon it was just me and the trees. I sighed, completely content.

Once near the school, I saw someone jogging toward me. I squinted to see who it was. Why, it was my good old pal Dustin. Well, there went my peaceful state of mind. I stopped walking and turned, heading the other way. Too late. I could sense him next to me. I kept going, keeping my head down. He shuffled his feet and cleared his throat. Still, I insisted on not starting the inevitable conversation.

"Uh . . . hey," he mumbled.

I stole a glance at him. Was it me, or had he grown taller? He was also in dire need of a haircut. I noticed that he was staring at me, so I quickly flicked my eyes back down. When I decided to look up again, he caught me, smiling shyly.

"What are you doing here?" I grumbled.

My question caught him off guard. He began to stutter. "I-I . . . Umm . . . I came to . . . to say hi."

I pursed my lips. "Well, you said it, so you can go away now."

He fell into stunned silence for a minute. Then he spoke yet again. "I was thinking that maybe we could go for a walk. You know, since we kind of already are?"

I sighed. We soon passed the boot camp. I have to say, I wasn't going to miss it at all. Not one bit. Only a crazy person would want to go there a second time. Even though I had gotten used to the pain, I was still sore. And if I moved a certain way, my leg muscles hurt like crazy. So no, I wouldn't go back if you paid me.

The silence was killing me, reminding me way too much of that horrible dream.

"Aren't you going to ask me a whole bunch of questions?" I asked.

"Oh, yeah," he said.

Then he unloaded all of these questions on me. I answered them without looking up, talking to my shoes the whole time. Some of them were stupid and others were reasonable. I answered them as best as I could, happy to be making noise. Finally they ceased. Again there was an uneasy silence between us. I longed to end it, but I couldn't think of anything to say. I didn't have to.

"Will you just look up at me?!" Dustin yelled in exasperation.

Jumping, I quickly looked up. He had stopped in his tracks to glare at me, nostrils flaring. If this was supposed to scare me, then it wasn't working. *Comical* would be the better word for it. I couldn't help but laugh. For some reason, I found his frustration really funny.

"What's so funny?" he demanded, still glaring.

I didn't answer, unable to quit laughing. He asked me if I was OK, anger gone. In its place was an expression of bewilderment. He took a step toward me.

The fit of giggles abruptly stopped. Without thinking, I gazed directly into his eyes. I was reminded of that look of pain and fear I had seen in those same eyes. That lifeless heap in my arms. No, that wasn't the real Dustin. That had been the dream Dustin. But if it had just been a dream, then why did it bother me so much? I turned away.

"Are you OK?" he repeated, taking another step.

I stepped back, snapping out of it. "What? Oh, yeah, I'm fine. Let's keep moving." I began to walk briskly down the path, hoping that he wouldn't follow, but he did.

Trying to keep the conversation light, I mentioned that I had met his friend Marcus.

"Really? Cool guy, isn't he? I think he loves to dance almost as much as you do."

"I know. I danced with him," I said gloatingly.

"You did?" he gasped, taken aback.

I shrugged. "Yep. What, are you jealous?"

He brushed this off with a flick of his hand. "No. What's there to be jealous about?"

I grinned. For a while, nothing could be heard except for the crunching of the gravel under our feet. I studied our surroundings. Where were we, anyway? There was nothing but trees and more trees. They were leafing out now, and some of them were flowering. Buds covered the ground. It was all very beautiful, but my shoulder had started to ache from the pressure of the bag I was carrying. All I wanted to do right now was go back to my room and get some rest. Maybe, if I was lucky, I wouldn't have that dream again.

"We should probably be heading back," I said, beginning to turn around.

Dustin reached out to stop me. "Wait. Just a little farther. I want to show you something."

With a sigh, I put my hands on my hips, eyes in slits. "What is it this time?" I tried to emphasize my annoyance. Here he was, keeping me from getting some rest after a very hard few weeks. Honestly, I didn't think I had any patience for this at the moment.

He noticed this and laughed. It was a loud playful sound. I couldn't help but crack a smile.

"Don't worry. You won't be disappointed," he promised, speeding up with me right on his heels.

We came to a stop at a square building. The words *The Hang Out* flashed in big bright red letters. Next to the building was a parking lot that appeared to be empty at the moment. Dustin sauntered right through the double doors.

He beckoned for me to follow. While going in, I noticed a sign stating that the area was closed. I pointed this out to him. He told me that it just meant the place was reserved.

"For who?" I asked, already knowing the answer.

"For us, of course," he replied, wiggling his eyebrows.

He traipsed over to the switch panel. With a flick of the switch, all was transformed. My eyes were seriously bugging out. To our left was a huge arcade. To our right there stood a restaurant. We faced a skating rink. It must have had at least a mile-long perimeter. Dustin headed for the stairs. I hurried to follow.

He walked on up to the skate booth. He climbed over the counter and disappeared between the rows and rows of skates.

"What's your size?" I heard his muffled voice ask.

"Size 6," I answered, too stunned to say anything else.

He soon returned with two pairs of skates, one for me and one for him. "You have small feet."

Ignoring him altogether, I went back downstairs. We sat on little benches in the middle of the room and put the skates on. Then we entered the rink. I shivered, wishing that I had a coat. It was freezing cold in there, like we had gone back in time. Goosebumps had already appeared on my skin. Dustin handed me a scarf, gloves, and jacket as if he had read my mind.

"So, do you know how to skate?" he asked as I gratefully slipped the winter garments on.

"I've skated before, but be forewarned. I'm not very good."

He shrugged. "Neither am I, but that doesn't mean I don't like to skate. Come on!"

I let him lead me out onto the ice, watching my footing. Dustin skated really fast compared to me. He practically melted the ice with his speed. I rolled my eyes. What a show-off. Keeping a steady pace, I scowled at him as he zipped past. The whiz boy jumped and twirled around the ice. He reminded me of those professional skaters I used to watch on TV with my mom. Every leap and turn was perfect and beautiful, like watching a dancer, only in colder climates. For a moment I stood mesmerized by the skater in front of me. When he noticed me staring, he grinned, starting to skate over. I abruptly turned away, wobbled a little, and focused on skating. Slow and steady. Side to side.

Dustin was soon beside me, matching my slow and steady pace. Neither of us talked for a few minutes. There was just the sound of our skates scraping the ice.

"You like my skating," he commented.

"I thought you said you weren't good. Are you kidding me? You're awesome! Have you thought of trying out for the Olympic team?"

He blushed. "Thanks, but I think I'm too young to try out, anyway."

I snorted. "Young shmung. Once they see you skate, you're so in."

"Thanks," he said again.

I shrugged. "It's the truth."

Suddenly Dustin took my hand and had begun pulling me toward the middle of the rink.

I quickly grabbed hold of the railing, stopping him in his tracks. "What do you think you're doing?"

"I think I'm about to teach you a few tricks, if you don't mind," he calmly replied.

Shaking my head, I told him that I could barely skate, much less do tricks. I would fall flat on my face.

A smile tugged at the side of his mouth. "That's not going to happen. I won't let it. Now, let go."

Taking a deep, exasperated breath, I reluctantly did as he asked and allowed myself to be pulled away. Once we were in the middle of the rink, he dropped my hand and skated around me in a tight circle.

"I'm going to teach you how to spin," he explained. "Keep one foot on the ground and use your other leg for momentum. Try to keep your body facing me, no matter what."

I nodded, concentrating on what he said. After a while of slow spinning, Dustin sped up a bit. He kept getting faster and faster until he had turned into a blur. I twirled and twirled, gathering speed along with him. Wait a second; I was going way too fast! There seemed to be no way to stop myself. In a panic, my eyes darted around the rink. Worst thing I ever could have done. This only made me really dizzy. I closed my eyes, attempting to stop the dizziness, but I was caught off balance. Before I knew it, I was flailing my arms, trying not to fall. However, the force of gravity prevailed. I was going down.

Just when I was about to crack my head open on the hard ice, strong hands stopped my descent. I opened my very tightly closed eyelids. They rested on a boy's foolishly grinning face looming over me. Dustin.

"You all right?" he asked, laughter in his voice.

I glared up at him. "Yeah, sure. A few more seconds and I so would not have been all right."

He rolled his eyes. "You were never going to fall. As I've told you before, I wouldn't let that happen."

Like I could totally trust him. I stood up, pushing his hands from around my waist. "After everything that's happened, you of all people shouldn't expect me to just trust you."

He backed up away from me, looking hurt. "I know. Sorry."

Shoving his hands into his pockets, Dustin resumed skating.

I stayed where I was. Although I felt guilty for snapping at him like that, my words were true. I skated over to the benches and took off my skates, stripping off the winter wear.

I headed upstairs with the skates slung over my shoulder. During all this, Dustin kept skating, not even noticing my absence. This didn't surprise or upset me. I didn't really feel like speaking to him, anyway.

Once upstairs, I put the skates back and took a look around. Directly next to the skate shack was a big Starbucks. It had to be one of the nicest ones I had ever seen. Waves of the wonderful, intoxicating smells of coffee beans and pastries floated from the restaurant. Next to that stood a seriously creepy-looking laser-tag maze, which I so wanted to explore. Since I had no intention of asking Dustin, I let myself in.

The place was pitch black except for the neon lights. Laser guns and glow-in-the-dark vests hung from hooks at the entrance.

I decided to take a gun and vest for safety reasons. You'd think I'd freak out holding a laser *gun* and all, but I didn't. They were just toys. What was there to be afraid of?

I cautiously walked down the dark path. Flashing signs warned me to *Beware* and *Watch Out!* Then I felt something move under my foot. A second later a skeleton flew out in front of me. I screamed. My screams soon turned into laughter. Just a dummy, of course. This was like a haunted house. Whoever came up with that must have been very creative. Every few minutes a creature of some kind would jump out in front of me. So that I could pass, I had to shoot them with my laser. I had fun, but the experience would have been better if someone else was there with me.

Right on cue, someone or something came up from behind me and grabbed my shoulders. Strange, I couldn't recall stepping on a trigger. Yelping, I whirled around. Instead of a mechanical creature, a snickering boy stood before me.

"How did you find me?" I asked.

Dustin shrugged. "Wasn't that hard."

"You scared me."

His eyes gleamed under the flashing neon lights. "That was the point."

I shot him with my laser gun. Grinning, he ran into the dark. I hurried after him, but the maze had swallowed him up. Using my laser as a flashlight, I crept along, searching.

He came out of nowhere and grabbed me, scaring the living daylights out of me. Shrieking, I wriggled out of his grasp. He laughed, shooting at me with his laser gun. We went on like this for a while, darting behind walls, giving each other a scare, and of course, shooting. Then we exited the maze and headed for Starbucks.

Once we had reached the counter, some guy popped right up without warning. He had on a Starbucks tee and cap. Flashing a very charming smile, he asked us what we would like. His teeth were so white that they had to be veneers. This was interesting, because the guy couldn't have been any older than twenty. The tag on his shirt read *Jeremy*. His eyes were a pretty blue. They reminded me of the beach, my favorite vacation spot. Wavy locks of dark hair hung loose from under his hat. Boy, was he cute.

Since I was too busy staring into Jeremy's eyes, Dustin ordered for me. When the cutest employee in the world handed me my iced mocha latte, his fingers touched mine for a second. They were pleasantly warm. I would have fainted right there if Dustin hadn't been steering me away from the counter. I stole another longing glance toward Dreamy Jeremy. He gave me a small crooked smile. My heart did a little flip.

Dustin sat down across from me in a booth. I could tell he was kind of annoyed by my sudden crush on the employee.

"Where did he come from?" I asked, gazing in his direction.

Dustin shrugged, taking a sip of his Frappuccino. "I don't

know. He started working here a few days ago. It's not that important." He was trying hard to hide his irritation, but he wasn't doing a very good job.

Then I took a sip of my first latte ever. It tasted really good. I hurried to take another sip. Then another. Dustin laughed at my reaction to the tasty beverage.

"Haven't you ever had one of those before?"

I shook my head. "Nope. This is my first." I took another long sip before I went on to say, "Wow, this is so good. Mom says I'm too young to . . ." I trailed off, looking down at my cup.

He cleared his throat. "Sorry. This was supposed to get your mind off of . . . you know."

I smiled weakly. "That's sweet, but that's not the only reason why you brought me here."

He sighed, running a hand through his hair. "Actually, there's something I need to tell you, about that building we saw on the tour."

I remembered the strange calmness on that little girl's face and shuddered.

Moving closer, he began to tell me what he'd found out.

The building had turned to be some kind of science lab, as we had already assumed. Different experiments were performed on a selection of kids. Usually they came out mentally and physically traumatized. On very rare occasions they were mostly fine, with just a few bruises. However, they all lost memory of what had happened. Dustin's dad visited the lab daily, checking on the progress. This was all Dustin had gathered so far.

Dustin put his head down on the table. "Lily, what if I was wrong about Dad? What if he really is insane?" He raised his head to rest his troubled eyes on me. "There are other things I've heard too. Really bad things, like sometimes, for a test, he has kids commit murder. Just to see if they can do it. I may have even witnessed it happen without knowing. I think there's something really wrong going on, but there's no way to know for sure."

"Well," I said, placing a hand on his, "there just might be a way."

Eyes alight with curiosity, he leaned in closer. "What?"

I flashed him a wicked grin, the idea already forming in my head.

TRAGEDY

Dusk had fallen, casting an eerie shadow upon the whole campus. The only sources of light were the streetlamps that bordered the park pathway. Everything was at a standstill and quiet. So quiet it sent a chill down my spine. The air had grown cool, menacing. A more than gentle breeze tussled my hair, played with the flaps of my jacket.

We stood side by side, staring at the looming fortress. Just the sight of it gave me goosebumps. I wanted nothing more than to turn right back around, but I was determined to see this through.

Dustin shifted uneasily beside me. "Are you sure you want to do this?"

I nodded slowly. "Positive. Let's go."

We crept toward the lab building, as silent as mice. Dustin led me around to a side door. He took out a shiny gold key he had somehow managed to steal from under his father's nose. The door opened with a soft click.

We stepped into some sort of utility room. Brooms and buckets cluttered the floor. Other cleaning supplies filled the shelves. I pushed my way through the junk, reaching out to open yet another door. Heart in my throat, I cautiously turned the knob. Both Dustin and I held our breath.

To my relief no one stood waiting at the other side. Just a plain hallway. From the inside, the place strongly resembled an office building. The carpets were a dull gray, while the walls had been painted beige. Just like outside, complete silence.

I had just turned to ask Dustin which way he wanted to go when we heard voices coming in our direction. Quick as a whip, he pulled me back into the closet, leaving the door open only a crack. A group of guys in white lab coats passed by us. They seemed to be in the middle of some kind of heated debate. Their words were precise but fast. I couldn't catch anything they were saying.

Since they were deeply engrossed, I decided to follow. Dustin tried to stop me, but he wasn't fast enough. He had no choice but to hurry after me. Neither of us said anything for fear of being heard. We simply trailed the arguing scientists at a near tiptoe.

After taking a few winding turns, they finally stopped at a large metal door. The word *Restricted* had been painted in bright yellow letters. One of the lab coat guys pulled out some sort of keycard, waving it around in front of what appeared to be a scanner. With a mechanical beep, the door creaked open.

Once they were all inside, it slowly began to close. This was my last chance. I dove inside before it was too late, tugging Dustin along with me. We landed on our hands and knees. Thankfully, the clueless scientists were already on their way, their backs facing us.

We stood on the balcony of a large warehouse-type room. The floors were made of cement, the walls a dirty gray. Scientists swarmed the area. Many were walking in and out of a large glass cubicle that stood right in the middle of the room. I struggled to see what was inside.

Taking a closer look, I realized that three sides of the cubicle had built in walls. Only the side facing us had been left as glass. Both the walls and the floor were an unnaturally clean shade of white.

After a few minutes, only one lone scientist stood in front of the glass. He appeared to be pressing buttons on a control panel of some kind.

While he messed with the thing, a door at the far right side of the warehouse opened to admit yet another group of scientists. This time they appeared to be wheeling somebody in on a stretcher, a child. They walked right into the glass cubicle. One of them held a syringe in her hand. Slowly she hunched over the sleeping child and pressed it into his arm. Almost immediately the boy awoke with a jolt. The woman whispered something in his ear. Dutifully he stepped down from the stretcher.

With a large mechanical swooshing sound, all the doors to the mysterious glass room began to close. Red lights flashed. All lab workers began to evacuate the cubicle, leaving the boy to stand there alone. They all stood and watched. He stared right back, a mixture of fear and grogginess frozen on his face.

Nothing happened for a few seconds. They all just stood

there, waiting. I used those few seconds to study the boy. He had to be about ten. His hair was a vibrant shock of blue. His nose was slightly crooked, as if it had been broken at some point. He wore a white T-shirt and pants. Not a speck of dirt could be seen.

Several seconds went by and I had started to wonder if they were just going to stand there all day, when the boy suddenly cried out in pain. He crumpled to the floor, curling up in a ball. He began to shake and quiver like he was having a seizure. His skin turned a frightening shade of green and then switched to red. He appeared to be stretching, growing about a foot a minute. His arms continued to expand into the arms of a buff bodybuilder. The veins were nearly popping out of his skin. The groans of pain turned into roars of rage. During this whole transformation, no one made a move to help him. They simply stood there.

The boy looked up. Lips curled into a snarl, he slowly stood up. He no longer resembled a scared little ten-year-old boy. That boy had disappeared. A livid monster had taken his place. Beating his chest, the beast let out a mighty roar. The guy holding the control panel pressed a button. Out of nowhere, a large silver object came racing toward the monster boy. He swatted it like a fly. As the thing fell to the ground, I realized with a jolt that it was a car. They started coming faster now. Again and again he pummeled the cars until they were nothing but scrap metal. He never tired. Whatever they threw at him he would simply crush into smithereens. Every time he destroyed something, another button was pushed, and whatever wreckage that was left would simply sink into the floor.

Finally, after about fifteen minutes, the monster began to show signs of tiring. His reflexes had become slightly slower. Some of the things were starting to hit him. Although he still roared and fought ferociously, small cuts were accumulating on his tomato-colored skin. One piece of scrap metal got him smack against the head. He fell with a bang. He struggled to get back to his feet, but it was too much. By this time a large gust of wind had been added to the storm of flying cars. Giving up entirely, he held his hands up in a feeble attempt to protect himself.

As if triggered by this sign of defeat, he started to shrink back to his original size. His arms became weak kid arms again. This turned the odd man-made storm deadly. It slowed, but not enough. Frantic, he tried dodging the large objects, but his now normal legs weren't fast enough.

By the time the onslaught stopped, he lay trapped under a car. Only his arm stuck out from beneath the beat-up vehicle, utterly still. The glass doors slid open, red lights flashing. The same scientists who had wheeled him in rushed to remove him from under the car. They carried his broken body out, not even bothering with the stretcher. Blood seeped onto their once perfectly white coats. The boy showed no sign of life. He simply lay limp in their arms.

Once they had left the room, a few of the other scientists seemed to be writing down notes on pads of paper. The man standing in front of the control panel glanced up from his checklist.

"Bring in the next one," he called.

Sick to my stomach, I turned to Dustin. He stood frozen, unmoving except for his hands. They were shaking like crazy. His eyes remained locked on the glass cubicle.

"Dustin?" I touched his shoulder.

He did not blink or move. It was like he couldn't even see me. I shook him. Still he didn't move. Suddenly I heard the familiar mechanical beep of the door behind us. I pulled Dustin behind a corner, pressing our bodies against the wall. Once whoever it was had their backs to us, I shoved Dustin through the door and soon followed.

Without talking, we made our way back to the utility room. Thankfully, the halls were quiet as we made our escape. Dustin silently opened the door to the outside world. He didn't say anything as we headed for the school building.

Finally I couldn't take it anymore.

"So, do you wanna talk about what just happened in there?" I shot a nervous glance in his direction.

"There's nothing to talk about," he mumbled.

I frowned. "Of course there is. That kid just turned into some kind of beast right in front of us. And then he-" I bit my lip, unable to say the words. "Don't you have anything to-?"

His head snapped up, eyes glistening with what I presumed to be tears. The question died in my throat. The expression on his face confused me. He was livid, full of a hatred I had never seen before.

"There is nothing to say," he spat. "My father is a sick, twisted man and I can't believe I thought he was a good person. Almost all my life, I've been working for a monster!"

He turned away, taking a shaky breath. "You were right all along. I'm such an idiot. And do you know what the worst part about this is? I was probably the one who brought that kid in. And now he's . . . "

Something wet ran down his cheek. He wiped it away. Before I could say anything, he had broken into a dead run. I called after him, but he was already gone, having disappeared into the night.

PLAN B

For the next few days, I searched for Dustin, but he was nowhere to be found. Since I no longer needed to take karate, there was no contact between us during the day. That space in my schedule had been filled with Advanced Combat 101. Luckily, True and Cattie had also been upgraded to that class. Although I couldn't talk to Dustin, I could talk to them.

Right before class, I told them what Dustin and I had found out, and they were utterly shocked. I talked them into changing our plan. We weren't the only ones that needed to get out. Those kids being used as human guinea pigs were in dire need of a breakout, too. Both were skeptical at first. How would we even be able to do this without being caught? I didn't have an answer for that one, but I did know this was the right thing to do. However, they were right—we couldn't do this on our own. We needed help. And I finally figured out where to find him. Instead of going to my next class, chemistry, I headed straight for Dustin's rooms.

You read this right. I said *rooms*. Dustin had a whole side of a building to himself. He had one big room for sleeping, then a whole series of them for studying, hanging out, watching TV, playing the latest video games. All that good stuff.

He was reading when I entered his bedroom—a room I had tried to avoid, but this was serious. I needed his help. Since he appeared to be completely engrossed in his book, I decided to play a little trick. Creeping closer, I stayed as quiet as a mouse. Once close enough, I let out a bloodcurdling scream. Jumping up with surprise, Dustin fell right out of bed. The book flew out of his hands.

"Wha-what's going on?"

I laughed. "That's what you get for disappearing."

Dustin glared at me. "You're crazy, Lilith Mason." Shaking his head, he laughed too.

Then he asked me what I was doing there anyway, since I was supposed to be in class. I threw the same question back at him.

He sighed, rising from the floor and taking a seat on the edge of the bed. I stayed where I was, waiting.

"When I saw what they did to that kid, I just lost it. All I could think about was that hand sticking out from under the car. I couldn't focus, so I decided not to go to class. Sorry I didn't warn you or anything. I just needed to process everything." He looked up.

The memory of the monster boy made me shiver. I remembered the blood. So much blood. This made up my mind. We had to get those kids out now, like tonight. He shook his head, claiming that this was impossible to do on such short notice. Besides, where would the kids go?

"Away from here, of course! You know how to drive. So use your mad driving skills and get them out. Maybe to the nearest hospital or clinic. Then they would be able to get checked out."

He looked up at me, unsure. "Do you really think we can do this?"

I grabbed his wrists. "Yes, I really do. Please. Will you help me?"

The silly boy shook his head in disbelief. "You're pretty sure of yourself, aren't you?"

Dropping his wrists in disgust, I let out a huff of exasperation. "You bet I am. I can't just sit here and do nothing while more innocent people are being treated like lab rats. Really, where's your common sense?"

"My common sense is telling me that we can't do this tonight. It's impossible. Maybe we can in a few days or so, but not tonight."

"Well, you're wrong!" I shot back with a glare. "I'm going to do this with or without your help. Since it looks like you already have your mind made up, then I'll just show myself out."

Dustin stopped me before I could make a dramatic exit. "All right, I'm in. But before we start planning, I need to excuse you from class. Trust me, if any of the teachers think you're skipping their class, there will be severe punishment."

I started for the door. "Let's go then. No time to waste."

Dustin hurried to keep up with my fast-paced walk, telling me to slow down. I would not, however. This was very important and I didn't want to lose too much time when we could be making our plans.

When Mrs. Lorgnette, the chemistry teacher, saw us, she excused herself from class and stepped out into the hall. "Lily, there you are. Where have you been?"

Dustin stepped forward. "Excuse me, ma'am, but something has come up and I need Lily right now. Here's a letter excusing her from class. Could you please give this to the other teachers so that they know she's absent?" He handed her the note, tapping his foot impatiently while she read it.

She looked up at him, then at me. We smiled angelically back at her.

Mrs. Lorgnette sighed. "Fine, but you're responsible for the work you miss."

I answered her with a "Yes, Mrs. Lorgnette. Thank you." My teacher sighed again as she went back to her classroom, closing the door behind her.

Letting out a quiet whoop, I pumped my fist in the air. Then I hurried back the way we'd come, Dustin at my heels. He'd gotten a little used to my brisk pace. Good. There was so much to do in so little time.

Once in his room, I ripped paper out of the back of my notebook and took a pen from my pocket. I sat down on one of the beanbag chairs, hand poised to write. Dustin sat across from me. He laughed at me for being so secretary-like, but I didn't laugh along. Once he saw that I meant business, he cut the laughter and began to strategize.

This is how it was going down. Dustin would convince his dad that he wanted to take me out on a date. That way nobody would be suspicious if we were gone for a few hours. Before leaving, Dustin would somehow obtain the map for the lab building. How? I had no idea, but he assured me that it was no problem at all. Next, we'd find True and Cattie and be on our way.

Using the route we had taken before, we'd break into the building, find the kids, and get out as fast as we could. Then Dustin would bring around the getaway car. (His dad had some kind of secret stash of cars somewhere.) If all the people didn't fit, then we would have to make second and third trips. True and Cattie would stay with whomever was left and keep them hidden until we came back.

After dropping the kids off at a hospital . . . Well, we weren't sure what the logical thing to do would be after that. I mean, if we released just the kids from the lab, wouldn't they just take more kids from the school? That would totally be defeating the purpose. And another thought. What would happen to us? It would be way too suspicious how the timing of our departure matched the timing of the breakout. Of course, we were hoping that we could save the kids as quickly and quietly as possible, but there really was no telling what would happen.

Dustin and I both paused, thinking about what to do. I wondered what I was going to do after we'd saved everyone. Dustin had to have gotten the hint that I was planning to escape with them. What if he tried to stop me? Would I have to use the gun lying at the bottom of my bag? The most important question was, would I be able to? The memory of that horrible dream made me flinch. I quickly went back to figuring out how to get my peers out of the school and back to their families.

Dustin snapped his fingers. "I think I know what to do."

I leaned in to hear what he had in mind. He spoke excitedly, making hand gestures while he explained. I sat there and listened, impressed. He knew more about this place than he had let on. I took notes. My pencil flew across the paper, using up a big chunk of my notebook. We looked over what I had written, made some changes, and that was that. We had our plan.

"So I'll talk to Marcus about it and see if he knows anyone he can really trust that's willing to help," Dustin promised as I got up to leave.

"Yeah, and I'll ask the girls." I decided to ask Cameron too. That is, if I could find her . . .

He smiled. "OK. This just might work." He sounded surprised.

This annoyed me a little. "Of course it will. With geniuses like us, anything's possible."

He laughed. "I guess you're right. See you tonight."

I turned to go, but then I remembered something. As I passed the school building, I noticed something odd. In faded white letters, the title *Wackerson Academy* had been painted on the front of the building. I couldn't believe I hadn't noticed it before.

Dustin smiled an embarrassed little grin. "Guess I forgot to tell you . . ."

I took a step toward him. "What?"

His grin grew even wider and more embarrassed. "My last name isn't what you think it is. It's actually Wackerson."

Somehow this did not surprise me in the least. "I guess that makes sense."

He gawked at me. "Really? O-OK. Anyway, he's comfortable with using his real name because this place is a real boarding school. Some of the kids here are just coming for the schooling. Their parents have no idea what this school really is."

I sighed. "That figures. Are there any more secrets you feel like sharing before I leave?"

Shaking his head he replied, "Nope. You know just about all my secrets."

I smiled. "I'm sure that's not the case." With that, I made my exit.

BREAKING IN

Butterflies filled my stomach. I had no desire to eat the food on my plate, but I needed the energy. Without tasting anything, I chewed and swallowed. I kept going over the plan in my head. It was frightening to know that in less than an hour, I wouldn't be going over it, I'd be *doing* it.

True, Cattie, Marcus, and some other kids sat across from me, clearly thinking about the same thing. Earlier that day, I had talked to True and Cattie about the events that would be taking place that night. They were all for it. I hadn't been able to get a hold of Cameron. She must have been studying or something, because I couldn't find her. Oh well. I hoped she did well. Anyway, the people that I could get a hold of met up with me at the dining hall. Marcus had brought his most trustworthy friends. He had told them all about the breakout. So there we sat, picking at our food. When it was time to go back to our rooms, we didn't dare look at each other. It would have given too much away.

I immediately began to get ready once I reached my room. This "date" had to look convincing, so I combed my hair and tugged it into a neat ponytail. I picked up the crimson dress

I had found carefully laid out on my bed. I decided to wear shorts and a T-shirt underneath. That way I'd be able to take it off once we were out of sight. I pulled them on and checked myself in the mirror. It really was a beautiful gown. How could his father possibly have known that it would fit me perfectly? Doreen must have had a hand in picking it. The dress would have matched my glasses if I hadn't gotten contacts from the optometrist on campus. It also went well with my skin tone. Apparently red was my color. Turning my head from the mirror, I closed my eyes and took a deep breath. Time seemed to be closing in on me. In a matter of minutes, I'd be out of this room forever. At least, I hoped it would turn out that way.

When I opened my eyes, there was a knock on the door. This was it. I looked in the mirror one last time. I wasn't sure I liked what I saw. First, I looked like a frightened rabbit. Second, there was a hardness in those two eyes staring back at me that I hadn't noticed before. I flexed my arms. Were those muscles? How much had this place changed me? Before I could take a closer look, there was another knock on the door. This one was louder and more impatient. I hurried to answer.

Dustin's nervous face greeted me. He began to talk as I opened the door. "Jeez, Lily. Why were you taking so lo—?" He stopped mid-sentence and stared.

I squirmed under his gaze. "Sorry."

He blinked. "No, that's okay. Really. You weren't . . . I mean, I was just being . . . You look . . . wow."

I smiled. "Thanks, but we really should be going now. What's in the bag, anyway?" I gestured in the direction of the huge duffel bag he had slung over his shoulder.

He blinked again. "Oh. Well, I brought some gadgets that will help. A lot."

"May I see them?" I asked, getting a little impatient myself.

Dustin gave his head a little shake. It reminded me of a dog shaking off water after a bath. "Of course." He walked swiftly past me into my room, dropping the bag onto my bed. I unzipped the bag and took out what looked like a gun. I flung it back down. "Is this really necessary?" My nose scrunched up as if I'd smelled something awful.

Dustin rolled his eyes. "Don't worry. It's not an actual gun. Just a tranquilizer."

Gasping, I exclaimed, "We have tranquilizer guns?"

He nodded with a look like I was the dumbest girl on the planet.

I whirled around and strode toward my own bag. With my back to Dustin, I gingerly picked up the horrible object that had been concealed under clothing. It felt heavy and chunky in my hands. I slowly turned around, holding it out as far away from myself as I could.

All the while Dustin had been watching me curiously. His mouth dropped when he saw what I was holding.

I flashed him a nervous smile. "Guess we won't be needing this, then."

"How the heck did you get that?" he questioned.

"It doesn't matter now," I answered quickly. "All that matters is that we need to get those kids out. Now. So let's go."

We decided to take the other gadgets out once we had gotten to the meeting place.

On the long trek there, Dustin just would not drop the fact that I had a gun in my possession. He kept asking me silly questions. Why did I have it? How had I gotten it? Did I even know how to use one correctly? What was I thinking? Who had been dumb enough to give me one? That question smarted a little. All that really mattered was that I wouldn't have to use the gun. The relief I felt was the best feeling I had ever had at that school. No longer would I have to worry about having to hurt anybody with it. No longer did I feel like I was deceiving Dustin. That dream was nothing but a fading memory now. I could not help but skip and twirl with elation. Was it me, or was the setting sun brighter than usual?

My nagging friend picked up on my sudden giddiness and ceased with the flood of endless questions. He crossed his arms, eyebrows raised. His walking slowed. I slowed down too, almost tripping on my dress. It was beautiful, but irritatingly long.

"You seem happy," he commented, glowering at me.

I laughed at his annoyance, which made his scowl deepen. "That's because I am happy. I'm happy that I don't have that thing anymore and that we're going to free everyone."

Dustin wouldn't quit with the glaring. "You should've told me."

"I'm just gonna tell you the whole story so that you don't have to keep asking me questions."

After I explained the plan we created at boot camp, there was a long silence. He didn't look at me. His eyes met nothing but the dirt path. We were almost at the meeting place.

"Say something already," I begged, lightly touching his arm.

Dustin moved away. He stole a quick glance at me. "You should've trusted me. If you had told me that you wanted to go home, I would've figured out a way to help you."

"Ha!" I snorted. "Yeah. Right. I've been telling you I wanted to leave ever since I got here! Now I'm supposed to believe that you were willing to help me? That's a bunch of crap and you know it."

He frowned at me. "Excuse me for thinking that maybe you were starting to like it here."

My laugh came out angry and sharp. "Like it here? Are you serious? I miss my family, my friends, and even school. And I mean my real school. Not this Wacko Academy or whatever it's called. You may not have an actual life, but I do."

OK, maybe I shouldn't have said that last part, but I was furious. He had no right to just assume that everything was fine now. What, was I supposed to spill my guts out for him and tell him how I felt? I had already cried in front of him, and big surprise, I was still here.

I didn't bother looking at his expression. His silence said it all. He knew I was right. With a snort of disgust, I ran away from him. Thank goodness I was wearing sneakers instead of high heels. It was bad enough I had to lift my long billowing skirts to run. Now I knew how the girls felt back in the olden days.

It's funny how fast your mood can change. When the walk had started, I was as happy as can be, without a care in the world. Now, as I ran the final distance, there wasn't an ounce of joy left in me. Anger had filled its spot. How dare he upset me before we had to go save everyone?

I could see the parking lot for the skating rink. My legs slowed to a brisk walk. To my great irritation, Dustin was not far behind. He caught up with me once I placed my hand on the door handle. He grabbed my shoulder to stop me from going inside.

"Look, I'm sorry. I was just a little surprised that you didn't trust me a little more. That's all."

I stared at him long enough to make him look away. "Why?"

He was taken aback by this simple question. "I just thought . . . we were, you know, friends." He said this haltingly, not meeting my gaze.

"Not unless friends lie to each other all the time," I answered.

Dustin's eyes met mine. "You're right, again. How about we agree not to lie anymore. Not to each other at least. Sound good?"

I allowed myself a smile. "Yeah,"

We went inside, the fight officially over.

True, Cattie, Marcus, and the rest of the gang were waiting for us at a booth in Starbucks. I couldn't help it. I searched in vain for the cute employee. Sighing, I followed Dustin to the table.

They greeted us rather cheerfully for people who were about to perform a risky rescue mission that could end badly.

Once Dustin had put the bag of gadgets down on the table, it was back to business. He took out a few tranquilizer guns.

There were enough for each of us to have one. Next, he took out the same little silver box he had taken out of his pocket the night I was captured. He explained to everyone that if you pressed the green button on the side, the box would unfold and expand into a ladder. There was only one of those, and since he was the only one that really knew how to use it, Dustin kept it. Next were the stink bombs. He had been able to get his hands on only a few of these, so we couldn't all have one. He handed us each security cards to wear around our necks. They would allow us to get past any scanners.

"Now this," Dustin began, holding up a small black thing, "is an earpiece that will help us communicate. Each of us will have one." He handed them out.

The earpiece felt really weird. It was really cold against my skin and it felt like I had a plug in my ear, like the ones kids wear for the pool.

Dustin then handed me a walkie-talkie. He told the group that both he and I would have them as a backup to the earpieces. After that, he took out a few more gadgets that he thought might help us. Then came the map. Everyone seemed surprised that he had been able to get his hands on it. He spread it out on the table, looking smug. The greatest thing about it was that every nook and cranny of the building had been marked. It showed the hidden doors, windows, and rooms. Everything.

"How in the world did you get this? I mean, this has all we need. It must have been really hard to find," I marveled, studying the detailed map.

He shrugged. "No big deal. All it took was some brainpower."

I shook my head in disbelief. "After this is all over, you've gotta tell me how you got it."

He grinned mysteriously. "Deal."

I turned back to the map. "Looks like we can enter this way." I pointed to the spot. "Then we split up, find all the kids we can, and try to avoid the mad scientists."

Taking a pen out of my purse, I marked all the escape routes. Then we assigned hallways to people. It was decided that we would go in pairs: me and True, Dustin and Marcus, Cattie and some guy named Gilbert, then Kathleen and Carlos (more of Marcus's friends). With everything decided, it was time to go.

True slowed to a walk beside me on the trail. "Do you think we might still use Mission Impossible IV?"

"About that . . ." I told her that I'd always known I couldn't shoot Dustin, and that I'd already shown Dustin the gun, and how Dustin had reacted.

She looked thoughtful for a minute. "You sure you made the right call?"

"Yes," I answered simply. To tell you the truth, it really was as simple as that. Like I told Dustin, deep down, I knew that I was never really ever going to go through with the plan.

True nudged me playfully. "You like him, don't you?"

I raised an eyebrow. "Excuse me?"

She laughed. "Stranger things have happened. Anyway, it

sounded like you two had a little somethin' going on back home."

"That was back home. We're here now . . . and just friends. Sort of."

True nodded slowly, not really believing me. She took the hint and dropped the subject. She noticed my dress for the first time, stating that it was one of the prettiest dresses she had ever seen. Why wear it now? I explained to her that I had only worn it because I hadn't wanted to arouse suspicion. It had to look like I was going on a date with Dustin.

"How did Dustin react when he saw you wearing *that?*"

I shrugged. "He acted a little goofy, but it's no big deal."

True laughed. "You're acting like you don't care, but you know you do. I know what he was thinking. He was thinking that you looked totally hot in that dress, which you do, by the way."

Rolling my eyes, I thanked her, but assured her that Dustin definitely was not thinking that. Besides, I wasn't going to break into a building wearing a dress, no matter how good I looked in it.

Up ahead of us, Cattie was talking poor Gilbert's ear off. He was being very polite, standing there and nodding his head at whatever came out of her mouth. The look on the boy's face was in between confusion and polite interest. The others watched this ordeal, trying hard not to laugh.

Finally we arrived at the lab building. It looked even more uninviting and sinister than it had before. A dark cloud loomed over the tall, plain building. I shivered. This was it.

This was what all the planning had been for. Time to take action.

The group gathered by a couple of bushes. I began to take off the dress.

"What are you doing?" Dustin asked in alarm.

I told him that I was taking off the annoying dress and not to worry. I had clothes on under it.

"Oh." (Did he sound a little disappointed?)

I folded it up and left it behind a bush, straightened out my shirt, smoothed my hair, and casually walked back to the group.

"OK, people. Let's get this show on the road," I said, clipping the walkie-talkie to my shorts pocket.

Everyone nodded solemnly. Dustin took out the carefully folded map. We did a double check to make sure everybody had their gear. And that was that. We were off.

Before we could go inside, Marcus had to freeze the security camera. That way the people watching the video wouldn't see us. Once he was done tinkering with the camera, Dustin took out the golden key again. He searched for the side door, but strangely, couldn't find it. Neither of us understood where the utility room could have gone. It had definitely been there a few days ago.

While we tried to figure these things out, True wandered around the building. She searched for the invisible window that had been marked on the map. She signaled us with a loud clear whistle. She had found it.

We quietly made our way to her. Her hands seemed to be sinking into the wall. The sight was kind of unsettling. True felt around the window, trying to find the opening. Then, with a cry of triumph, she tugged upward. Suddenly a perfectly square-shaped hole appeared where a wall used to be. I cautiously glanced inside. There was a big desk with a few chairs surrounding it. A chalkboard filled with calculations and scribbles that no one but a genius could understand made up the wall across from the window. This was likely where the evil scientists had their meetings.

Signaling for the others to follow, I climbed in. Being the last one in, Carlos closed the window. It turned back into a brick wall.

"How the heck did they do that?" Kathleen wondered in awe.

Dustin shrugged. "Some sort of hologram or something. With all this money, the technology has to be super advanced." He acted really bored about this, like an invisible window was nothing special. Was he kidding?! This stuff was so advanced it was futuristic.

"According to this"—he held up the map—"we're in the boardroom. And right out those doors are two hallways. I guess that's where we split. Let's move."

We followed him out, praying as we passed through the doorway that no alarms would go off. Fortunately, our prayers were answered. Wiping sweat from my brow, I quietly closed the door behind me. Once at the fork in the hallway, we re-formed into two groups of four rather than pairs. I ended up being with True, Dustin, and Marcus. Cattie would be with the other group. I felt kind of bad for her since she was working with people she barely knew. My pity wasn't necessary. Cattie seemed perfectly at ease with them. I couldn't help but feel relieved. Don't get me wrong. She was a good friend. It was just that she could be kind of annoying at times and I really did not need a distraction.

"Remember, open every door with caution. Don't hesitate to use the tranquilizer guns," Dustin reminded everyone before we split up. "OK, the earpieces are on. So if you need anything, just press it to your ear and start talking. We should be able to hear you. If you need to turn it off for any reason, just remove it from your ear and it will shut down instantly."

After the "good luck's" and "see you later's," my group took the left while the other took the right. Our hallway looked almost exactly like the one we walked the other night, but there was no way to be sure whether it truly was. Ominous doors lined the walls. Each one held a secret that I was afraid to find out. Tranquilizer guns ready, the girls took one side while the boys took the other. Carefully, True and I opened the first door. It opened to a rec room. There was a big flat-screen TV, a few comfy couches, foosball tables, ping-pong, air hockey, and pool tables, plus a video game center. We checked everywhere, but there was no one. The guys were the same. They had walked into a bathroom.

The rest of the rooms in that hallway were empty too. However, there were clues that people had been there recently. In one room was a rack of wrinkled uniforms. Some were dirtier than others, and a couple were ripped and had a few strands of hair on them. Every single one had the same fresh grassy smell. My guess? The children had been outside a little while ago. The question was, where were they now?

At the very end of the hallway stood a lone elevator. That was the only way up. No stairs. No nothing. The elevator was a dead end. This wasn't good. We didn't know what was up there.

Even though the alarms in my head were so loud that everybody had to be hearing them, Dustin took a brave step forward. He glanced expectantly our way. His strange calm with this whole thing was really starting to bug me. Just because he had nothing to worry about, being the head honcho's son, didn't mean that our lives weren't on the line here.

I sauntered right into the elevator, mimicking Dustin's coolness. Once by Dustin's side, I turned to the others. Two pairs of uncertain eyes met my reassuring gaze.

"Come on, guys. There's nothing to be afraid of." OK, even I didn't believe that. "We've gotten this far, so let's keep going. Besides, you know I've got your back."

"That goes for me too," said Dustin, stepping forward. "We're in this together. It's not just about us. There are a whole lot of people counting on us right now, so let's get up there before it's too late."

The others clambered inside after that little speech. Since there was bound to be a camera in there, Marcus busied himself by searching for and disabling it. Kind of his specialty. While True watched him in plain awe and admiration, I observed Dustin. His face showed determination and a touch of anger. I guessed that this was toward his father and the people working there. Hands clamped in tight fists and shoulders clenched, he stared straight ahead without really looking at anything. I came to realize that maybe the strange calm was just a front, hiding the fact that he was about to burst.

I touched his shoulder. He quickly snapped out of his daze and focused on the hand resting on his shoulder.

"Loosen up. We can do this." I flashed him a friendly smile.

His smile was more forced than mine. He still wouldn't look directly at me. "Sorry, guess I'm freaked about this whole thing. I mean, what if something goes wrong?"

"Don't talk like that. We're going to get these kids out of here, no matter what."

He looked away and muttered, "That's what I'm afraid of."

I glared at him in exasperation. Why did he have to be so pessimistic?

Dustin met my agitated gaze. Suddenly my eyes were unable to move. Seriously. My eyes were locked into place. We stared at each other for a very long time. Well, at least it felt that way. His beautiful chestnut eyes bored into mine. I tried to find something in those eyes, like in the books, but it was like he was blocking me out or something. There was nothing. Just a sea of brown. All I noticed were the creases and shadows under them, indicating that he hadn't been sleeping very well. His eyebrows were smooth and shiny. A stray lock of hair spiraled down just over his eyelid, threatening to get caught in his long eyelashes. I fought the urge to reach up and put the lock back in its place.

This I took in without moving or blinking. I started to wonder if he was going over my face like I was going over his. The thought made me a little self-conscious. Of all the things to be worried about, I was worried about how I looked to him. Was my hair a mess? Were my clothes wrinkled? Dear Lord, were there zits on my face that I hadn't seen before? My eyebrows furrowed. As if he had been worrying about the same thing, Dustin's did too. We grinned at each other. This time both smiles were genuine.

Then the elevator door opened. I had to rip my gaze away from him to see what lay ahead of us. It was another long hallway, which looked even more menacing than the first one. Something was different about this hallway. I could feel it. Carefully and slowly, I stepped out with my tranquilizer gun raised. The others followed.

Just like before, we split up in pairs for each side. Me with True and Dustin with Marcus. The first door was locked. It didn't have a scanner either, just a lock. I had taken a pin out of my hair and was just about to put it in the keyhole when there was a click and suddenly the knob began to turn. Both True and I jumped back, pointing the tranqs at the door. A man and a woman walked out, both wearing starch-white coats.

The man was saying something to the woman. Something about running more tests. Then they noticed us. Surprise flashed on both of their faces. The man held his hands up. The woman reached for something. Before I could so much as flex my forefinger, True had gotten them both. They sank to the floor, fast asleep.

Dustin and Marcus ran out of their room, saying that they had heard voices. Then they saw the two people on the floor, little needles sticking out of their necks.

"Did you do that?" Dustin asked, looking over at me.

I shook my head. "Nope. That was all True. She has some seriously fast reflexes."

Marcus gave her a friendly slap on the back, nearly sending her sprawling onto the floor, but she kept her balance. "Nice."

She blushed. "Thanks."

After we had dragged the two unconscious scientists into a closet, we went our separate ways again. Since the door had so nicely been opened for us, we strode right in. We gasped when we saw what was inside. Shelves full of chemical and medical bottles surrounded us. There were syringes in a big bin on the far side of the room. While I stayed where I was, True roamed the room. She examined the petri dishes that had been placed on the long table taking up the middle of the room. Her expression became confused and horrified at the same time. I came over to see what was wrong.

The petri dishes contained oddly colored liquids. Each one had been labeled with words that I couldn't even pronounce. True took some gloves out of a container by the syringes and snapped them on. She ignored my stare and tossed me a pair. Then she picked up some dishes and brought them closer to her face. She sniffed one that had a lime green liquid in it. She hurriedly put it down, gagging.

"Don't smell them!" I hissed in alarm. "You could seriously hurt yourself."

My curious friend wasn't listening. She was already picking up a different, even brighter colored one. I rolled my eyes in exasperation and started rummaging through the papers laid out on the table. They seemed to be some kind of charts, each one headed with a person's name. Under each name was their age, weight, height, gender, and blood type.

Then there were spaces for notes. The scribbles that I could read mostly talked about how much medicine was given to them and how they had reacted. Then there were hypotheses on what would happen if they were given a higher dose. After this came the observations and conclusions. A lot of them didn't sound too great. The reactions could be really repulsive. One note said that the child became covered in swollen red blisters. Another one said that a girl's skin began to peel right off the bone. Some were so horribly disgusting, I'm not even going to repeat them. I eventually put the charts down, holding my stomach.

True looked up from her petri dishes. "You OK, Lily? You look like you're going to be sick."

I turned away from her. "I'm fine. Let's please just get out of here and move on. We've been in this room for too long."

The boys stuck their heads inside, wondering why we were taking so long. When they saw the shelves of chemicals, their jaws dropped.

"What is this?" Dustin asked, eyes sweeping over the room.

"I don't really know." I replied. "On the table there are lists of names with, like, information about stuff. They . . . they said what happened to them after they got certain doses of drugs."

Everyone looked at me closely, expecting me to go on. I didn't go on. There was nothing to say. The look on my face told it all.

Dustin's jaw clenched. "We have to hurry."

The next door had a scanner. We had all decided to go in together just in case there were people in there. Dustin took the keycard from around his neck and waved it around in front of the scanner. There was a beep. Then the door swung open.

Inside there was a huge window. Behind it was a big room that looked a little bit like a skating rink. Only there wasn't any railing, or ice for that matter. The walls were starch-white like the coats on those sorry excuses for scientists. Even the floors were strangely blank. It was a bigger version of the glass cubicle we had seen in the warehouse room.

Marcus muttered, "What the heck?"

There were some kind of controls and buttons by the window. Keypads. Different words were on the buttons: *Strong Winds, Crushed Cars, Gunfire, Earthquakes, Flood.* The buttons had been grouped under headings like *Speed, Strength,* and *Agility.*

Gently touching the pads with my still-gloved fingers, I answered, "This is one of those simulators the scientists use to run the experiments."

On the left side of the keypads were what looked like video game controllers. Curious, I moved them around. With a sharp ping, machinery began to come out of the white room's walls. It moved in whatever direction I moved the controls.

"Cool," I heard True say. She reached over to push a button. Before she could touch one, Dustin's hand shot out to stop her. She looked up at him, startled.

"Don't touch a thing," he warned, fiercely glaring at her.

Scared now, True removed her arm from Dustin's grasp and backed away.

Through clenched teeth I suggested that we leave. So we all left the room, careful not to make a sound.

Out in the hallway, Dustin signed to us to split up again, in different teams this time. While True and Marcus went down the hall ahead of us, Dustin and I followed a little ways behind. This gave me opportunity to be mad at him. I flicked him in the head. His hand flew up to his head.

"Hey, what was that for?!" he exclaimed in surprise, struggling to keep his voice low.

"What do you think?" I shot back. "Look, I know this is stressful and all, but that doesn't mean you can take it out on True."

His excuse was that she could have compromised everything by touching a button. People could have heard something or detected it and then we would have been done for. I reminded him that I had touched the controls and nothing bad had happened. True had been a big help so far and was risking her very life by being on this mission with us.

Dustin didn't say anything. He just turned his back on me to open the next door on the left, while Marcus and True were opening the one on the right. He seemed to be having trouble picking the lock, so I gave him a gentle (OK, maybe not so gentle) push so that I could pick it myself. I had it open in about ten seconds. Enough said.

A whole variety of rooms greeted us from behind the door. In one room, there was a big desk with family pictures and the kind of office phone that has a bunch of different buttons. The other rooms resembled hospital rooms. They even had that unnaturally clean hospital smell.

The first room was empty. In the second room, however, lay a little girl. Closer up, I saw that it was the same girl I had seen being wheeled into the building. Her hair was cut shorter and she appeared to have aged somehow. Her eyes were ringed with purple, like she hadn't slept in ages. There were yellow spots all over her transparent skin. She moaned in her sleep, calling for her mother.

I lightly touched her forehead to wake her up. Her eyes flew open instantly. Her hands shot out to form an iron grip around my wrist.

"What do you want from me?" she asked in a frightened tone.

"To get you out of here," I answered simply.

She gazed up at me, eyes wide. "I can go home?"

I nodded. The girl stared at my outstretched hand for a minute. Then, after some coaxing, she let me lead her out of the room.

Dustin was waiting for us. When he saw that I had a companion, he smiled. He knelt down to the little girl's height and introduced himself. Honey practically dripped from every word and she ate it right up. Dustin gave the girl a small rubber ball he pulled out of his pocket.

"What's your name, cutie?" he asked her gently.

"Brianna," she replied in a shy voice.

"Brianna," he echoed. "That's a pretty name."

She just blushed, casting her eyes down. Honestly, I felt like barfing a little bit. Just a little. I mean, he was going a bit over the top.

I knelt down beside Dustin. "Brianna, can you tell me if there's anyone else here?" My voice wasn't quite as sugary sweet as Dustin's, but it was gentle.

She pointed to the room across from hers. "There's a boy in there. I don't know what's wrong with him."

Dustin went in while I stayed with Brianna. In a minute he came out with a boy around the age of ten. The boy's hair was a coppery red with streaks of dark brown. He wore the same white sweats as the girl. He stared sheepishly at the both of us through his purple-lined eyes. As he came closer, I noticed that there was something wrong with his arms. They were oddly deformed and hung limply at his sides.

The boy saw me staring and sighed. "The bones in my arms have turned to mush, so they're useless." Then he heaved an even heavier sigh so full of despair it was heartbreaking.

"Do you know how that happened?" I asked.

He shook his head, explaining that all he remembered was being led into a dark room and forced onto a gurney. The rest was a blur.

I had more questions, but Dustin cut me off. "We really need to move on. Is there anyone else here?"

The boy said that he wasn't sure. We searched the other rooms and found three more children: two boys and one girl. One of the boys, Brandon, had horrible red warts all over his body. Lucas's hair was the brightest white I had ever seen. It fell in thick locks down his back. Unfortunately, it wasn't only sprouting from his head. The weird-shaded hair grew out in patches on his arms, legs, knuckles, and eyelids. Seriously. His lashes were mad long. The girl, however, was worse off than all of them. Her skin looked like it was sliding right off of her. For some unknown reason, it held on. Her eyeballs were nearly popping right out of their sockets.

The girl stared at me, her face permanently droopy. The only way I knew that she was a girl was because of her long wavy hair. It was too pretty to be a boy's. Her eyes were a deep, calming blue. Whenever one of us tried to speak to her, she'd just stare at us with those sad eyes.

Once we had found everyone, Dustin and I briefly explained our plan. They listened intently with solemn expressions. Surprisingly, the children didn't have any questions, ready to follow any orders given.

We cautiously stepped back out into the hallway. True and Marcus stood right outside the door along with four other people. One of them looked to be about a year older than us. Another was quite small. Too small. The older one's skin glowed a sickly green. I tried very hard not to stare.

True smiled at our little group and greeted them cheerfully. Marcus eyed them with uncertainty. I couldn't blame him. They were quite a sight. Besides True's greetings, nothing was said. The others stayed eerily quiet as we led them down the hallway. They spoke only when spoken to, as if this was the olden days or something.

While going from room to room, the group of children increased. By the next elevator, we had a group of fifteen. Each one had a terrible deformity of some kind. Was it me, or did the injuries get worse as we went on?

On the elevator ride, I once again took the time to study Dustin's facial expressions. He appeared to be both sad and angry as he scanned every face. Without warning, his jaw dropped in horror. His eyes widened. Before I could follow his gaze, he had flicked his eyes down with a guilty expression.

"What's wrong?" I asked.

He didn't look up. "I think I know some of them." His voice was the saddest I had ever heard it.

Tilting my head in confusion, I said, "Yeah . . . So . . . ?"

Dustin looked up, angry. "So that means I brought them here—and that means whatever happened to them is my fault. Just like that boy." He frowned. "I'm such a creep. No, I'm worse than a creep. I'm dirt. Filth. Garbage. Scum . . ." He continued to insult himself.

I winced at some of the words he used. Jeez. He was being really hard on himself.

He was still muttering insults as the elevator door slid open to yet another long hallway.

"I know where we are," one of the kids said quietly. We all turned to see that it was Lucas who had spoken. "This is where they bring us for experiments. I'm almost sure of it." A shiver went through the whole group.

Shoulders tensed, I stepped out into the hall. The others followed a little reluctantly, but they followed. As before, Dustin and I and a handful of kids would investigate the rooms on one side while our two friends and their charges took the other.

With sweaty palms, I slowly turned the knob of the first door, which strangely didn't have any lock. Sure enough, it was a cold, dark room with an operating table standing under a single fluorescent light. Next to the table was a platter of needles that had been placed on a tall metal stand. The needles were of every shape and size, each filled with an oddly colored liquid. The whole scene looked like it had come straight from a scary science fiction movie.

The boy with the deformed arms, Theo, turned pale. Lucas stared at the needles, growing sicker by the minute. Brianna grabbed hold of Dustin's arm, burying her face in his sleeve like she couldn't bear to see any more. The rubber ball he had given her remained clutched in her right hand. I noticed that she was holding a lot tighter than necessary. She seemed to have a little crush on him. I didn't really think anything of it since she was so young. With no reason to linger, we left quickly.

The next door stood ajar. We were all hesitant to go in. Dustin slowly pushed the door open with his foot. The rest of us filed in after him. The room was very similar to the other. It would have looked exactly the same if there weren't people inside. A man stood hunched over the operating table. He hadn't noticed us come in, for his back was to us. He remained focused on the frail girl that lay before him. The careless scientist grabbed a random needle without so much as a glance the tray . He moved to stick it into her arm, where a vein would be. The unconscious girl was oblivious to what he was about to do to her. We all stood there watching in astonishment.

Before I could think twice about it, I shot him right in the back. He whirled around to face us, eyes wide. He quickly pulled the tranq needle out of his back, saw what it was, and gasped. The man stared at us in bewilderment. Suddenly his eyes became unfocused and he toppled to the ground, out cold.

I briskly stepped over him to examine the girl, while the others remained paralyzed. To my great surprise, I didn't see just any girl. I saw Cameron.

ESCAPE

I stood over the operating table, paralyzed with shock. Dustin appeared next to me. He let out a cry of horror when he saw her. Hands slightly shaking, he touched the side of her neck to make sure she was alive.

"Lily, I can barely feel a pulse," he said quietly. "We need to get her out of here. Now." The look on his face told me that he was dead serious.

Without another word, he gingerly picked her up. He carefully wrapped her limp arms around his neck and laid her head against his chest. Dustin shivered a little.

"She's so cold." His voice was thick with distress.

It took all of my strength to keep myself from bursting into tears. This could not be happening. Cameron was one of the kindest people I knew. She had done nothing wrong. Still, there she lay in Dustin's arms, barely breathing. I was afraid to know what had been done to her already. Was it because she was supposed to be The Girl, but it didn't work out? I kicked myself for not paying more attention when I could no longer find her. Something should have gone off in my head. How could I have been so clueless?

The group of kids stared at Cameron as Dustin carried her out of the room. Nobody said anything. We just silently followed him. He didn't even glance at the other rooms as he trotted down the hallway. His eyes were too busy studying Cameron.

Marcus and True emerged from a room on the other side of the hallway. They both looked at Dustin, then at me, with alarmed expressions. All I could do was shrug and trot after Dustin.

I grabbed his shoulder, forcing him to stop. Our group of kids came to a stop behind us.

He turned to glare at me. "What?"

I didn't shy away from his intense stare. "I know we need to get her out of here, but we need to figure out the fastest way to do that."

He nodded. "You've got a point. Take out the map."

Dustin and the kids crowded around me as I spread it out onto the floor. I found where we were and searched for the marked exits. Just as I found a nearby window, there were voices coming from down the hall. Whoever it was would be turning around the bend any minute now. If they saw us, we were dead meat.

We ran to the window, careful to stay quiet.

True caught up with us. "What's going on?" She kept her voice low, because she had heard the voices too.

I flashed her an apologetic smile. "I'm so sorry, but there's no time to explain. Keep looking for kids and we'll be back as soon as we can. But for right now, hide."

She was still confused and clearly wanted to ask me more questions, but she simply nodded sharply, gave me a quick "Good luck," and hurried to tell Marcus what was going on. I ran to follow Dustin and the rest of the crew.

I found them standing in front of a blank patch of wall. Brianna was in the process of feeling the wall for the hidden window. Once she found it, she quickly opened it and stuck her head out. When her head came back in, her little eyebrows were scrunched in worry.

"It's kind of high up."

Dustin took a peak out the window. He fumbled in his pocket for a second. Then pulled out the small metal box. He pressed the button on the side and threw it to the ground outside. As I knew it would, a ladder unfolded itself right before our eyes.

"I'll go first," he said. Then he awkwardly climbed out with Cameron still in his arms.

One by one, everyone climbed down until I was the only one left. Just as I put my leg out to climb down, there was a beeping sound and the ladder disappeared, folding itself back up into a box. I fell back, staring at the ground in terror. Without the ladder, it was a really long way down. Dustin had carefully handed Cameron over to Lucas (who was startlingly strong for a boy his age) and began to fumble with the box.

He looked up, confused. "It won't go. I'm sorry. It does that sometimes."

Of course that would happen when it was my turn to go. Just my luck. So there I stood, frozen. The voices growing louder every second.

"Jump! Don't worry, I'll catch you." Dustin called up, holding his arms out for me.

The sound of his voice jolted me out of my stupor. I quickly took a stink bomb out of my pocket and threw it behind me. Swallowing hard, I eased myself out of the window. Closing my eyes, I said a silent prayer begging God not to let me go splat all over the ground. I heard someone cry out. They were here. It was now or never. Without opening my eyes, I let go.

To my relief, Dustin caught me. He wobbled a little, but held on to me. I slowly opened my eyes to find him staring down at me. He fought a grin.

"What's so funny?" I snapped.

He shrugged. "Nothin'."

Narrowing my eyes, I ordered him to put me down. He hesitated for a second as if he was contemplating whether to obey or not. Then two men stuck their heads out the window, coughing uncontrollably and holding their noses. Shouting, they began to climb out. Dustin quickly set me down, took Cam back into his arms, and had begun to run before any of us could even blink. We ran helter-skelter after him with the two men still shouting after us.

Dustin reached the getaway car in no time. He put Cam in the back, then hopped in the driver's seat and started the engine. Our pursuers had given up a while ago, calling backup instead. But we needed to get out of there fast, before backup came looking for us. Everyone piled in, with me in the passenger's seat and the rest in the back. Dustin zoomed off the second we were all in.

"Wait. How are we going to get through the force field?" I asked as we went speeding toward the exit.

"If we go fast enough, the car should go through," he explained, staring straight ahead. "I suggest you hold on tight."

It was obvious when we had hit the force field. There was a loud bang. We were all jolted back in our seats. The car shuddered violently. For a second I thought we were going to go flying back and that would be the end of us. However, we made it through.

Dustin didn't slow down until we were officially off the campus and onto the highway. The GPS said that we were about twenty to thirty minutes away from the nearest hospital. That was a relief.

"What will happen to us when we get to the hospital?" asked Theo after a while.

"I'm hoping the doctors will figure out what's wrong with you guys and fix it. And you can see your families," I said, turning my head to look at him.

He smiled slightly, uncertain hope spreading across his face. I smiled back at him, getting a little hopeful myself. We spent the rest of the ride talking about each other's families. Dustin remained quiet, focusing on the road. But now and then a smile flickered across his face.

Finally Dustin pulled into the hospital parking lot. We ran into the ER. People stared at us wide-eyed and shocked. The nurse gasped when she saw Cam and the other children.

"I–I'll go get the doctor," she stammered, beginning to run down the hallway.

In a minute a doctor arrived, his white coat flapping as he briskly made his way to us. He did a double take, but didn't freak out like the nurse. The doctor calmly called down more nurses. Then he turned to face us.

"What happened exactly?" he asked.

Nobody really knew how to answer, so he decided to ask a slightly easier question.

"Do you know what happened to her?" He gestured toward the unconscious Cameron in Dustin's arms.

I stepped forward. "I think she's been injected with something. And—" I faltered. "And I think she's dying." The word hung in the air. There was an awkward silence among the group. Without warning, I started to cry.

Just then two people came running out with a gurney. They took Cam and rolled her away. Meanwhile, one of the other nurses rushed over. She sat me down, asking if I needed anything.

I looked up at her through blurry eyes. "Can you call my parents and tell them I'm OK?"

She smiled. "Absolutely. What's your phone number?"

Once I had told her, she hurried to use the hospital phone. I leaned my head back on the wall and closed my eyes for a minute.

Someone sat in the chair next to me and coughed.

"I wonder if she's going to be all right," Dustin said.

"She will," I said firmly, eyes still closed.

He sighed. "I'm not going back until I'm sure everyone's OK."

My eyes flew open and I jumped up. "Oh my gosh! I totally forgot about the others. They never even got back in touch with us. We have to find out if they made it!"

Dustin nodded grimly. "Let's talk to them on our walkie-talkies."

I walked out without another word. Dustin followed me out.

I leaned against the side of the building while he fidgeted with the walkie-talkies.

"Marcus, are you there?" he called earnestly.

Marcus answered in a muffled reply, "Yeah, I'm here. Where are you?"

"The hospital. Did you guys get out safely?"

True answered this one. "Yes, but barely. The rest were caught."

My jaw dropped. "What?!"

Her voice was sad. "We met up just before we got out, but those guards . . . me and Marcus were lucky to get out of there ourselves."

I didn't know what to say.

"Listen, they know we're here. I can hear the sirens right now. I don't think we can evacuate the rest of the school."

Dustin glanced over at me. I pursed my lips. She was right. The whole school would be impossible to penetrate now. Everyone knew what was happening by this time. It was over. My shoulders sagged in defeat.

"Just get out of there."

Dustin took the walkie-talkie. "Mark, remember when I taught you how to drive? Go to the garage and take a car. It's not hard. Trust me. There's a GPS in almost every one, so don't worry about that. Get there as fast as you can and DON'T GET CAUGHT."

"All right. See you, bro."

"See you soon."

Dustin and I stood there for a minute, staring out into the indigo sky. A couple of stars had appeared. We had failed, but neither of us wanted to say it.

"You taught Marcus how to drive," I commented, not knowing what else to say.

He shrugged halfheartedly. "Yeah. I just decided to one day. Guess it came in handy."

I laughed without smiling. "Yes, it did."

Police sirens drowned out whatever his answer was. About four or five police cars entered the parking lot at top speed. We watched in silence. Of course they had called the police. A group of mutated kids had just burst into the emergency room without any sign of an adult.

"We better get back inside," I muttered.

"Right," he agreed, heading for the door.

The kind nurse was just coming back from the phone call. She told me she'd just been speaking to my mom, who would be here soon.

She turned to Dustin. "Do you need me to call your family?"

He shook his head. "My family already knows where I am. They'll be here soon too." He sounded so confident, the nurse believed him instantly.

"I have to get out of here," he whispered as a police officer walked in.

"What! Why?" I whispered back, eyeing the officer, who was now talking to the nurse at the front desk.

When I turned around, Dustin was already backing away. "I'll be back," he mouthed, before turning and walking briskly down the hall and out of sight.

HOME AT LAST

And so I stood alone, watching both the nurse and the police officer shoot a quick glance in my direction. By now a few more officers had entered the building, forming a small crowd around the main desk. The first officer said something to the others. Now they were all staring at me, including the other patients. Feeling my cheeks grow warm, I looked away.

After more talking, one of them broke away from the group and walked toward me. He appeared to be in his early twenties, younger than the rest. I guessed he was chosen because of my own obvious youth. They believed that he would be able to get more out of me since we were closer in age. I noticed one of the badges on his chest read *Officer Hunter Davis*.

Once he had reached me, he removed his hat, revealing floppy brown hair.

He smiled, showing me that he meant no harm. "Hello there. What's your name?"

"Lily," I answered quietly, wondering what I was going to tell him.

Deciding to break the ice, he continued with more polite questions about my age, where I was from, and if someone had contacted my parents. Then he started in with the tricky stuff.

"Could you tell me how you got here?" he asked softly.

"I . . . I . . ." My mind was running a total blank. I had no idea how to explain to him what had happened. It was an unbelievable story. Besides, I didn't want to give Dustin away.

"Lily!" I heard a familiar voice shout.

I turned my attention away from the young officer to see my mother running toward me.

"I can't believe it. You're alive!" she cried, pulling me into a tight hug. I stood up to hug her back and buried my face into her shirt, breathing in her scent. She smelled like flowers and a pinch of cinnamon. Mom held me at arm's length to study me.

I was only slightly aware of the officer standing to the side, watching us.

"You've grown taller!" she marveled, tears still streaming down her cheeks. She was right. I was nearly her height now.

My mother gave me the once-over. "Where are your glasses?"

I laughed, explaining that I had gotten contacts.

She cocked her head to one side, eyebrows raised. "Hmm . . ."

I laughed again. "It's a long story. Where's the rest of the family?"

Mom smiled. "They're at home waiting for you. Let's get out of here."

At this time, Officer Davis stepped in front of us. "Ma'am, I assume that you are this girl' s mother?"

Mom nodded. "That's right. I'd like to take her home, if that's all right with you."

"I understand, but we're trying to figure out what happened here, and it appears that your daughter has a great deal to do with it. I'm going to need her statement."

My mother wrapped a protective arm around my waist. "Not without a lawyer. Look, we will do whatever you ask of us, but obviously my daughter has been through a lot tonight and needs some rest before she gives any kind of statement. Now, you have my word that we will be back first thing in the morning and then you can ask all the questions you want."

Officer Hunter looked thoughtful for a second, gears turning in his head. "That sounds reasonable, but I'll have to ask my chief first."

He made his way back to the first officer, who was now speaking with the parents of one of the mutated children. The two men talked a little and I thought I saw the chief give a small nod. The young police officer came back.

"You're free to go, but we'll need you back at this hospital by ten o'clock tomorrow morning to help us figure this thing out. Have a nice night."

My mother flashed him one of her most dazzling smiles. "Thank you, Officer."

We exited without a backwards glance.

When we arrived home, I was eager to see my dad, and yes, my siblings too. It was dead silent inside the house. I turned to Mom in alarm.

She got a funny look on her face, like she was trying hard not to laugh. "That's weird. Maybe they'll be in the dining room."

I couldn't figure out why they would be in the dining room, since it was only for special occasions, but I followed her into the room.

"Welcome home!" everyone yelled.

The whole room laughed at my shock. Our dining room was filled with family members and friends. There were streamers and balloons. A big banner read *Welcome Home Lily!!!* The dining room had been loaded with chips, cookies, cakes, pies, and other treats.

Malerie, Asialie, Amanda, and Ella ran up to hug me. Chase and Louis were close behind. Tears ran down my face in streams. I had missed them all so much. The girls were crying too. The guys hung back a little, not sure what to do. Laughing, I pulled them into a hug. They both hugged me back with ferocity. And was it me or were their eyes kind of wet too?

When the group hug broke, I eagerly searched for my dad, brothers, and sister. Once I had found them, I momentarily forgot about my friends and ran to my family.

I smacked into Dad at full speed, nearly knocking the wind right out of him. He stumbled back a little. Then he snatched me up into a bear hug. I curled up in his arms. He cradled me and held me close, just like he used to when I was little and kissed my forehead. I took a good look at him. His eyes glistened with tears. Everyone seemed to be crying because of me. Oh well. At least they were happy tears.

Aaron and Eric hopped around us, yelling my name. My sister was calmer than the crazy boys, but she still seemed ecstatic to see me. I left my father's strong arms to hug them. They were all talking to me at once, asking me questions and giving me the scoop on what had gone on in my absence.

Grandma Imani came to greet me. (I later learned that she had been there for a few weeks to support my mother.) There were more hugs and tears.

So I spent the rest of the night laughing and eating with my family and friends, happier than I had been in a very long time.

FAREWELL, FOR NOW

The next morning, my mom drove me to the hospital bright and early, as promised. We had gotten there earlier than the police, much to my relief. I still didn't really know what to tell them.

Dustin, Marcus, and True were sitting in the waiting room, tense and alert. They waved at me when I entered. I waved back. The nurse eyed Dustin suspiciously, wondering where he had been last night, I suppose.

While Mom talked to the nurse at the desk, I plopped down next to them.

"Sorry I left," I apologized.

True shrugged. "Don't be. You had to see your family. It's been nearly six months. Nothing to be sorry about."

The guys nodded in agreement.

"So how are the kids?" I asked. "Is everyone OK?"

Their expressions didn't relieve me in the least. Dustin cleared his throat and told us what they knew so far. The doctors were still running tests on Cameron. She had apparently been exposed to a number of dangerous chemicals. From what he could gather, the doctors didn't really believe that she was going to make it. But she was tough. She would show them all. She had to.

As for the others, Theo needed some kind of bone marrow transplant. They weren't sure what to do with Lucas. A vaccine was in the process of being made for Brianna. The girl with the skin problem was going to need major surgery.

I put my head in my hands. This was a lot to take in at the same time.

True patted me on the arm. "They're all going to pull through."

Glancing at her through my fingers, I asked, "Where's your family?"

She explained that her dad was coming for her.

My mom walked over to us. She informed us that we were able to see Cameron now, but only two at a time. Her family was supposed to be coming soon, so we had to hurry up.

Dustin and I followed a nurse to her room. She had been hooked up to all these tubes. She looked so small in that bed. Dustin rushed to her side while I took her hand.

"This is all my fault," he commented, staring at her unconscious face.

I reached over to put a hand on his shoulder. "It's not your fault. It's your dad's and those so-called scientists over there."

He shrugged my hand off. "That's true, but it's also my fault."

I gave up, knowing that he wasn't ever going to stop blaming himself. Cameron still lay there with no objection. I knew that if she were awake she would be setting him straight.

Maybe her getting better was the only way he would snap out of it. I stared at her for the longest time, willing her to at least twitch a finger or something. She didn't move a muscle. I sighed.

"The police want to talk to me about what happened," I said conversationally.

His head snapped up. "You can't tell them about the school."

I frowned. "Why not?"

"Because they won't find anything. A while back, one of my dad's associates got suspicious and tipped off the Feds. Everything was locked down somehow and all they saw was a normal boarding school. After that, Dad got rid of the guy. If you know what I mean." He dramatically ran his finger across his throat in a slicing motion. "Everything's already been locked down on campus."

Feeling a little sick, I asked, "What do I say, then?"

Dustin thought for a minute, and then advised me to say that I couldn't really remember. All I knew was that someone had threatened to hurt my family if I didn't come with them. I couldn't see the person's face since they were wearing a mask.

"When they test you," he continued, "they'll see that you were drugged. It's probably still in your system after all this time. That kind of stuff doesn't just go away."

I shook my head, reasoning that they would be questioning the others too. Besides, it didn't add up. We had just come into the hospital with a group of horribly mutated kids. I had to remember something.

He nodded. "You're right. Tell them the people who kidnapped you were experimenting on children. You did what you could to get them out."

I had to admit, it sounded like a pretty good story, but I still felt uneasy about lying to the police. Couldn't you, like, get arrested for doing something like that? Well, it was either death or jail. Either way, the options weren't very good. I bit my lip, wishing there was another way to remain safe and be truthful.

"You know I'm going back, right? That's why I couldn't let them see me," Dustin said, changing the subject completely.

I looked up to see him frowning down at Cameron. It seemed as if he was concentrating really hard on something, like making her open her eyes. At that moment, he appeared to be much older. His expression was weary. The shadows under his eyes had darkened. He wore the same clothes he had been wearing yesterday. They were wrinkled and dirty. His curly hair was a tangled mop on his head. I had never seen him look so unkempt. It was unsettling.

"You can't go back," I objected, resting my free hand on his shoulder. "Your father will find out what you did and he'll hurt you."

He glanced at my hand, then looked up at me with a sad smile. Sunlight coming in from the windows made his already beautiful eyes sparkle and shine. I had never noticed it before, but he had light brown highlights in his hair. It gave him a little more life. It made him look more like himself again.

"Whatever he does to me, it won't be that bad. I can take it. He can't kill me. I'm the heir to his stupid business.

No matter how much he punishes me, I'm never working for him again. No more recruiting for me. I'm done."

I searched his face. He was serious. Too serious for a teenage boy. Where was that sly smirk that got on my nerves?

"I want to go with you," I told him, even though I really didn't. I felt it was the right thing to do. The mission hadn't been fulfilled.

Dustin stared back at our sleeping friend. "No way." His voice sounded so cool and sure, it annoyed me. He had no right to make decisions for me.

Taking my hand off of his shoulder, I held my head up high in defiance. "You can't tell me what to do."

He managed to run his hand through that mop of hair and heaved a tired sigh. "Maybe not, but I'll try my best to stop you. Look, you just got back with your family. Do you really want to disappear again?"

My head went down an inch. "No," I said quietly.

"Anyway, my dad might not kill me, but I don't know what he would do to you. What if . . . what if you ended up like Cameron? Do you honestly think I could live with myself if that happened?" He looked up at me now, mortified by the thought. "Promise me you won't do that to yourself and your family. Promise you won't do that to me."

I tore myself away from his penetrating eyes. "Fine. I promise, but what about the others? They're still trapped there. And what about the school? They'll just take kids from there to replace the ones that escaped."

Dustin assured me that he would do everything he could to get them out. I wasn't so sure about what he would be able to do. Now that he had tried to help people escape, his father was going to have him on an even shorter leash.

The nurse came in to tell us that our time was up. Cameron's family had arrived. As we followed her out, the first one I saw was her brother. He looked to be about nineteen. He had the same eyes and hair as Cameron. Her dad was a balding man in his late thirties, early forties. His facial expressions were unreadable. The last to hurry past us was her mother. She was slightly heavyset and her frizzy red hair had been pulled back into a messy ponytail. Her face was red and blotchy from crying. She kept wringing her hands, a few tears still trapped in her eyelashes.

Neither of them noticed us as they scuttled after the doctor. When they had reached Cameron's room, I heard a loud moan from her mother and then weeping. The father was in the midst of trying to calm her down while her brother quietly identified Cameron as his sister. Then he and the doctor immediately began to discuss her condition. Someone closed the door and all was silent.

I tried to swallow the painful lump in my throat, but it wouldn't go away. A few stray tears ran down my cheeks. I brushed them away before anyone could notice. Well, Dustin pretended not to notice, but he didn't say anything.

We sat back down at our seats without another word. Seeing our expressions, True frowned.

"No change?"

We both shook our heads. She was just about to say more when a tall buff man entered the emergency room. He searched the room for a second, until his eyes settled on us. He reached us in a few long strides and towered over us with a morose expression.

True grinned. "Hi, Dad!"

Dad? I couldn't see the resemblance.

He cleared his throat. "Sweetie, would you like to leave now?" The word *sweetie* really did not go with his stature or his voice, which was deep and gravelly like a jazz singer's, only scarier.

She nodded. "Yes, I would."

"Wait," I said, touching her arm. "Don't you have to wait to talk to the police?"

She shook her head, explaining that she lived nearby and the police had already made an agreement with her parents. Her explanation seemed strange to me, but I let it go. I hugged True goodbye and promised to see her tomorrow at the hospital.

Once she had gone, the boys decided to go too. Like Dustin had said, he could not be seen. Marcus had flat out refused to let Dustin go by himself. I followed them to the door. This was it. I was never going to see them again. I hugged them both.

"Well, take care," Dustin mumbled, unable to meet my gaze.

"I'm going to miss you," I admitted. "Can you believe that?"

He snorted. "No, I can't."

I rolled my eyes. "Whatever. Just be careful. I wouldn't

be able to forgive myself if anything happened to you. So stay safe."

A ghost of a smile flickered across his face. "I'll do my best."

With nothing left to say, he turned and walked out, hands in pockets. I watched him go, unable to shake the worry.

Suddenly he stopped mid-step. He turned back around and briskly came back. I stared at him, wondering what the heck he was doing.

With a determined look on his face, he leaned forward and quickly pecked my cheek. His neck was all red, just like it used to be whenever he was nervous about something. My cheeks burned. All I could do was stand there with my mouth wide open.

"Goodbye, Lily," he whispered.

I blinked. "Bye."

With that, Dustin left for good. He was halfway to the car, where Marcus patiently waited, when I realized something.

"Wait!" I called, running after him. "You never told me how you got that map."

He smirked. "I will."

I frowned. "When?"

"When I see you again," he answered simply.

I smiled. "So you're saying that we'll definitely be seeing each other again?"

Laughing, he put his hands on my shoulders. "Of course we will. I do have to check on Cameron. Plus, I'll have to tell you when I free everyone."

My smile faded. "You can't do that all by yourself."

He shrugged. "Sure I can. I have Mark to help me. By the next time we talk, my dad's school will be officially closed."

I put on a brave face and tried to smile. Everything was going to be OK. It had to be.

"I'll be fine. Trust me," Dustin assured me. He looked me over one last time. Then he slowly leaned in to kiss my other cheek, not as quickly as the first time.

He dropped his hands from my shoulders and studied my face, trying to see my reaction, I guessed.

Casting my eyes down, I said, "Umm, I should get back inside before my mom comes looking for me. The police will be here any moment, so you need to go."

He was quiet for a minute, searching for words. Meanwhile, I mentally kicked myself for saying what I had just said. *Did you really have to mention your mom right now? Wow, Lily. Thanks for ruining the moment.* I gave myself another mental kick.

"Yeah. See you later," Dustin finally said. Then he turned and got into the car.

I watched him drive off and lightly touched my cheeks with the tips of my fingers. A wide grin spread out across my face. Malerie would so want to hear about this.

But first, I had a whole lot of explaining to do. With squared shoulders and a clenched jaw, I marched through the hospital doors.

FAITH WILKINS has been writing poems and short stories since she was seven. She loves music and plays the violin. She also sings in a local choral group called Jubilate. Faith began writing *Wacko Academy* during the summer of seventh grade in a spiral notebook. She currently attends high school and lives with her mom and two little brothers in New York's Hudson Valley.